"A riotous extravaganza,
ing, that goes over the t
loses its antic grace and s

"This is the most brilliant first novel I have read in years. . . . Rikki Ducornet's real talent is for language. She is a minor lord or lady of it, achieving abstruse comic effects by a kind of clowning classicism. *The Stain* is a very odd, accomplished and memorable novel by any standards."
—**Robert Nye, the *Guardian***

"A highly disciplined extravaganza. . . . The writing is highly impressive."
—***Times Literary Supplement***

"A tale of witchcraft, prostitution and sex . . . the images evoked in relentless detail recall Brueghel and Bosch . . . the atmosphere is steamy and pungent, indubitably a powerful nightmare vision."
—***London Times***

"An extraordinary black, erotic fairytale, an exuberant, touching and very funny novel."
—***Time Out***

"Ducornet displays distinct page-by-page talents (vivid imagery and invention) along the lines of Angela Carter."
—***Kirkus Reviews***

"Readers with voracious appetites for the bizarre may relish the spread prepared by Ducornet."
—***Publishers Weekly***

"A bold, Rabelaisian mixture of bawdy and horror, this first novel . . . is highly recommended."
—***Library Journal***

BOOKS BY RIKKI DUCORNET

NOVELS

The Stain
Entering Fire
The Fountains of Neptune
The Jade Cabinet
Phosphor in Dreamland

SHORT STORIES

The Complete Butcher's Tales

POETRY

From the Star Chamber
Wild Geraniums
Weird Sisters
Knife Notebook
The Illustrated Universe
The Cult of Seizure

CHILDREN'S BOOKS

The Blue Bird
Shazira Shazam and the Devil

The Stain

a novel by

RIKKI DUCORNET

Dalkey Archive Press

To the memory of Angela Carter:
once a shared place

First published in 1984 by Chatto & Windus in England and by Grove
Press in the United States.
First Dalkey Archive edition, 1995

Library of Congress Cataloging-in-Publication Data
Ducornet, Rikki, 1943-
    The stain / Rikki Ducornet. — 1st Dalkey Archive ed.
        p.   cm.
    1. France—Religious life and customs—Fiction. 2. Demoniac pos-
session—France—Fiction. 3. Girls—France—Fiction. 4. Birthmarks—
Fiction. I. Title.
PS3554.U279S7   1995   813'.54—dc20   95-16365
                                                      CIP
ISBN 1-56478-085-6

Partially funded by grants from the National Endowment for the Arts
and the Illinois Arts Council.

Dalkey Archive Press
Illinois State University
Campus Box 4241
Normal, IL 61790-4241

NATIONAL
ENDOWMENT
FOR THE
ARTS

*Printed on permanent/durable acid-free paper and bound in the United States of
America.*

aaa ooo zezophazazzaieozaza eee iii
zaieozoakhoe ooo uuu thoêaozaez êêê zzêêzaoza
khozaêkheudê tuxuaalethukh

—Jesus, the First Book of Jéou, from Werner Wolff's
Changing Concepts of the Bible (1951)

CHAPTER

1

Christ hangs above her head. His split chest reveals the exquisite knob of his ruby heart throbbing in a cage of thorns. His sepia visage brims with pathos and his open palms with blood. This image, tainted by persistent intimacy with humid walls, has also buckled; beneath its blemished glass the eyes mysteriously shine as from within a deep pool of stagnant water.

She cannot see Him. To gaze into those infinitely drear eyes she would have to lift herself and turn. This, in her present condition, is unthinkable.

Two other images adorn the wall: copper engravings of little broad-browed children in neatly buttoned boots and jackets. To the left and right of Christ they hang in tarnished frames and are titled respectively *Ne riez pas* and *Ne pleurez pas*.

On the bedside table stands a small porcelain figure of the Virgin Mary, the sort one brings back from Lourdes to accommodate a demiliter of holy water. Shattered and unsuccessfully mended, she is crowned with a little brown cork. The year of her purchase is visible on the faded ribbon that circles her waist: 1873. More than once, the man of the house in venomous fits of loathing has sent her crashing to the floor.

He is a hunter and leery of sacrament, at odds with life, at peace with Death—a banality he regularly pitches into the kitchen. He is replete in his meager vision, unquestioning and exempt from the blessed feeling the priest describes as "Awe."

Some die hard, they start and shiver; some die easy, just fall over. . . .

(She: "O Please! Please!" Holding her hands over her ears. And he: "You eat what I kill, don't you!" Pulling her hands away; kissing her hard upon her warm, full mouth.)

For this brutish soul she has given up everything. For this brazen, footloose, landless drunk (her father's words), living off the woods like a Gypsy, too good-looking to be honest.

Good-looking! Mean he is and savage, a mind like a clenched fist and a cock like a hammer; he has been rough with her, foul-tempered and surly. Good-looking! Those dark eyes of his are cruel! God damn him! She shivers, stroking her belly—swollen like the mounds which, scattered on the landscape, conceal ancient graves. She fingers the erect beak of her navel, her distended nipples, her breasts marbled green and blue, then childishly, hastily, makes the sign of the cross, crossing her eyes, fingers and toes for added luck, praying: Make the baby male! Then they would forgive her trespass. She hears her husband cursing in the kitchen. In the indecipherable mess that has accumulated over the past few days, he cannot find his left boot.

Not many months before, in the butcher's shop, as the butcher pulled a slab of dead muscle from a hook, he had stood behind her, mesmerized by her rump. Like her crazy mother who had danced at Mass as naked as a worm, she had a fine body and she had red hair. He imagined the red flags beneath her arms, between her legs—that symmetry. . . . To fuck a red-woman is to fuck a witch; she'll have power over you ever after, she'll suck the marrow from your bones, she'll dismember you, throw your broken body to the wind, hang your heart from a tree for the crows to eat; he has no book-learning, but these things he knows. His own mother has warned him of red-woman.

From her father she inherited the aristocratic nose. It recalled the old man's notorious stinginess. Finely arched, the nostrils delicately flared—it suited her far better than the old bastard. . . . She reminds him of his first hunt.

A boy of fourteen with a new knife, not a pruning knife, but a true hunter's knife—a Crowned Hand, curved and sharp enough to sever a windpipe—he ate with the men and he ate meat, not the thin gruel reserved for the women and children. He drank his coffee black and after, his mother had reached to embrace him, and he had turned away. His father said: A woman will bedevil a hunt like nothing else.

A killing happens fast. He remembers the rustling sound she makes in the trees and her startled look, the sound of the gun, the wound bubbling in her throat, her cry for air, the sound of her fall—of wood splintering. They drag her thrashing from the brambles; thorns are embedded in her hide. His father cuts into her and the guts slide from her leaping flesh, steaming. In this instant of ichor, of ruby, of shit and of diamonds, Life's terrible secrets are revealed to him. He is excited beyond belief, his eyes fill with tears. Death has given him himself. . . .

He could see her breasts beneath the tight black wool of her dress. And when she reached down into her apron pocket they pressed together, causing a deep cleft in the cloth. She felt his eyes scorching her flesh, hooking on to her body like prongs, his breath hot at the nape of her neck, the smell of him, the *heat* of him—making her shudder. And when she turned to go, one look had sufficed to impale her.

He, standing in her path, legs parted, forced her to brush against him. The meat in her hands bleeding into its grey paper.

"You like wild meat?" he said. "I'll bring you some game."

Ashamed, she blushed and dropped the parcel. It fell to the greasy brown-and-white tiles with an intimate slap. At once he bent to retrieve it, and as the butcher leered, expertly sawing marrow bones into wheels, he held her wrist and murmured into her ear the place—a certain stone at the edge of La Folie known as the Devil's Finger—she nodded, she knew, and the hour.

And she had gone. In fever. Slipped past the old bastard's bolted door, slipped from the cold house they shared in shame, in tedium and in silence. With her own small foot she had sprung the trap—famished, foolish mouse that she was! Perhaps he had bewitched her; the roots of sorcery are said to spring from sex.

For him she lost her honor, lost her inheritance, her name, burned all her bridges—for one instant of blindness beneath the stars and the naked eye of God! (Edma.) Had she been a whore, he would have taken her the same way, brutally, pushing her face into the earth.

When her pregnancy could no more be concealed, her father threw her from the house. Edma—a bloodhound with a nose for Disgrace—appeared on the scene just in time to water down her wayward niece with the kitchen slops. Her father, driven nearly to murder by this second act of disloyalty (his wife's insanity the first), kicked her down the stairs and, hanging to the cliff-edge of the stroke that would take his life within the month, silently threatened her with his umbrella. It was Edma who shouted—and loud enough for all the street to hear:

"You will burn! You and your brat, I swear!" Her anger so intense she spat, her white lips flecked with froth. "I swear . . . Satan will trample you both beneath his hooves! Whore! Whore and bastard!"

They married, although she had not asked for it, only for shelter. He offered; his reason fucked on wine (or so he argued later). Their witness was his drinking chum Arch-ange Poupin who, to her surprise, had been charming, gentle and even gentlemanly. He had composed a song for the occasion, and after the chicken dinner he had himself roasted in the fractured, gritty hearth, he sang it for her. And such was Archange's genius that, despite the bleak house, the bleak future and the fact that the bridegroom was very, very drunk, she dared believe—but only for as long as the song lasted—that she might find happiness.

The midwife, La Tatette, a sour-smelling crone as keen for the washing and dressing of infants as she is for that of corpses, has promised to appear later in the day with the unwieldy paraphernalia of her trade. Thanks to this woman —half saint, half hag—the mysteries of birth remain hidden from the eyes of the profane. The Evil Eye may appear any-where unannounced, but she is prepared to deal with it— better prepared for the Evil Eye, in fact, than for the ticklish terrors of a breech-birth, or the stranglehold of a treacher-ously wound umbilical cord. Her expected visit frees him, for although he would never admit it, he is fearful of his wife's misshapen body; in wine-soaked conceit, he imag-ines that the baby is a malignant growth.

Yet this morning, a surprising tenderness tugs at his heart and in amorous fellowship he sits down upon the bed be-side her.

"Little mouse!" he says, holding her small face in his rough hands. Her skin is so transparent he can see the veins branching at the temples. "Little Mamma!" But before she can answer he rises, disgusted with his weakness, and slam-ming the door behind him, gives his hunting companion— a patchy mongrel with unmatched eyes and an oversize head—a nasty kick in the balls. The dog howls and escapes through the open door and into the courtyard where, dash-ing around and around in diminishing circles, he frightens the horse, who—back-stepping—makes a terrific clatter upon the cobblestones. At that instant the baby wakes within her. It slams against her flesh with its small, soft skull.

She calls out but he is already gone; in expectation of the hunt the dog forgets his pain and barks joyously at the horse's side. And so she says to herself, flooded with foreboding:

It is the hooves that have awakened it.

All day she labored alone, for La Tatette was detained in La Folie by the early arrival of twin boys. Her pain—cyclical in the early hours—grew constant towards night, a raging moon orbiting within her, a drumming heart bristling with thorns.

He returned late, his boots heavy with mud. A fat hare, firm-fleshed and golden, hung by its ears from his belt. Even as he rode into the courtyard, he could hear her cries. She was wild, like a forest thing trapped, wounded and terrified. Her crazed eyes shone white, her spread thighs, the ravine of her sex and the heaving mound of her belly formed a monstrous landscape, not human, not of this world, the pit of Hell itself. And then she saw him. And she saw, dripping blood by his side, the dead hare. And as her baby spilled from her body she screamed, one brilliant blade of sound that—as a sword-tip breaks, striking bone—left a ragged edge of silence poised upon the air. So Charlotte was born. Born with the creature's image slapped to her face—a leaping hare, dusty plum in color, sprawled across her cheek, one paw scraping an eye and one her jaw. Covered with soft, velvety fur, it stood upon the flesh in relief.

He saw the Stain and thought it odious, and in that instant knew his wife would die, that even if he slaughtered a thousand thousand beasts he could not escape Death; that the hunter is himself hunted.

Blood was everywhere; he thought that the baby might drown in it and snatching it up discovered the cord, rubbery and wet. Confused, and cursing La Tatette loudly, he dropped the tiny, disfigured *femelle* he knew he hated, and gathering up all the linens he could find—mostly his own soiled shirts—attempted to staunch the flow.

La Tatette arrived at dawn. She found the three of them together in the room—the dead woman, the baby caked with blood and screeching, and the man dead drunk and moaning in a chair. She tied the cord which he had cut but left dangling, bathed the infant and wrapped it in a blanket; later she would feed it a thin soup of bread soaked in water which it would suck from her cold finger. She washed the corpse, pulling the soiled linens out from under it, wrapping it after in the stiff, clean sheets that had been stored in the chest for that purpose (along with a candle that once lit permitted the soul to find its way to Paradise; this candle also exorcised Thunder). Rolling the corpse from side to side she was able to make the bed, and he lay down upon the fresh sheets beside his dead wife. At once he slept, a heavy, sodden slumber, punctuated by ferocious snoring.

CHAPTER

2

The priest, a faded wood head secured by a black bottle body, rotates counterclockwise above the grave. Chanting unintelligibly between an unmatched set of porcelain teeth and sprinkling the coffin with a dubious mixture of holy water and spittle, he unlocks the invisible doors that opening one by one reveal the narrow entrance hall into the beyond.

"Mershyhashmershy, PishyushLord. . . ."

The infant reposes in her great aunt's gelid grasp. Edma is an ashen-fleshed female with rigorously ordered hair. Pulled into a silver sphere, it gleams at her temples like the polished prongs of steel forks, and reeks of violets. Emile, her spouse, droops meekly at her side.

"Ashesh to ashesh. . . ."

Emile, who has been staring fixedly into the pit at his feet, beams, and his clouded eyes clear momentarily. For there is one topic of conversation he may entertain with authority, overcoming his stutter and persistent anxiety, and that is: GARDEN PESTS AND HOW TO KILL THEM

> *Ashes he knows, ashes he loves,*
> *Ashes kill leek-worms, leeches and grubs.*
> (Charlotte)

With the same fervor with which Edma fights domestic and cosmic devils, Emile does battle with the leek-worm (that

14

treacherous guest who, in the calm of afternoons, secretly gnaws out the heart of Mother Nature's most venerable of vegetables), slugs and snails (generating spontaneously beneath the moon, their slime gleaming obscenely on the lettuce), Sicknesses of Degeneration, Tuberosities, Molds, rats and birds and—in berry season—small boys. His limited domain is boxed in by high walls of stone fanged with smashed bottles. From every tree hangs the mask of a scowling cat cut unconvincingly from flattened fish cans; everywhere are set out severed lead pipes, each harboring a store of poisoned grain; and every green thing growing is weekly doused in a bath of soapy water spiked with nicotine.

Ashes, poison, fire and knives,
Undying hatred and very sharp eyes.
(Charlotte)

If Edma's brow is marked with an expression of unremitting hatred for the imperfect universe, Emile's entire face has been grabbed and twisted into a permanent expression of astonished despair by the torments of vegetable and domestic husbandry. His face, his baggy pants shiny at knees and seat, his hesitant stutter, have made him the irresistible target for naughty boys who eagerly add to his miserable condition by tossing homemade firecrackers between his shuffling feet and throwing greasy luncheon scraps at him from the treetops.

Emile has only one testicle, but this does not account for the fact that until now the couple has been childless. Much later, as Emile lies helpless with fever, Edma will—to her everlasting satisfaction—discover his deficiency. And this after forty-five years of communal life. For not once will she remove her woolen underthings in her husband's presence; not once will he lower his pants in hers.

Woolens protect from drafts as does Humility and Silence (Edma to Charlotte, three years hence).

15

As soon as she is able, Charlotte will join Edma and Emile on recalcitrant knees upon the unforgiving linoleum of the kitchen floor—daily torture for Emile, a seasonal sufferer of gout. (But he never complains within hearing of Edma's protector, a waxen, underdressed God-image languishing silently in the chill air above the sink.)

The ceremony is over when the infant's father, his head luminous with wine, enters the cemetery. As the priest peers expectantly into the man's uncannily glowing face, and Emile tugs pensively on his own ear, Edma looks to Heaven, her nose wrinkling, as if detecting a bad smell. He, however, appears not to see them and in a haze reels past to the foot of the open grave where he stands swaying dangerously.

"Pig!" Edma shouts, savagely squeezing the baby to her unyielding breast.

"Hushsh! Hushsh!" the priest whispers, attempting to calm both Edma and the howling baby, and not very efficiently directing them towards the gate.

"Your teeth need fixing," Edma says to the priest as, upon taking her leave, she hands him the small yellow envelope containing his meager *pourboire.*

CHAPTER

3

The twins had come first, a presentiment, an annunciation. Their parents, Georgette and Georges Téton, simple folk who toiled for their bread in the hectic gloom of the local mushroom cellars, had the twins baptized even before the twisted cords of their dry umbilici had fallen. But even so, the Exorcist knew that the birth was his enigma. Boys and identical, mirror images, perfect polarity, they represented the two creative fluids: negative and positive. They stood beneath the Tarot's golden Sun, innocent and naked flesh branded by the nineteenth letter, the Hebrew *Quoph:* the ax, the knife, the sharp-edged weapon. Nutrition. Digestion. The Mineral Kingdom. The Téton twins slipped into the Exorcist's calculations as easily as a stolen coin slips into the mouth of a thief.

And as for the marked female, it was clear, after a night's feverish reflection, that she—trumpeted by the twins—was his *intended.* For did not the hare symbolize the Devil, the licentious moon and the female pudenda? And was not that signature visible upon her face?

He was the village Exorcist; he cured cancer with clay, and pimples with a crucifix dipped in chicken shit. The only man known to wear an earring, own a camera, to be seen at sunrise lumbering across the muddy furrows of freshly tilled fields, his black beard inking out itineraries, his black eyes darting to and fro like wasps, his tripod hanging from his shoulder like a strange wing.

The Exorcist loved order and hated fortuity. He believed in a patterned, intentioned Universe, mapped and pinned by Cosmic Hands. Unlike the Church Fathers, he did not argue that Evil was a lesser Good, a flaw festering like a boil on the buttock of Divinity. He knew Evil to be as Methodical as the Good, and so just as true. The Universe was like a great pie cut into two equal slices: one served up by Heaven, the other by Hell. And he stood in the middle. The discovery of his most unusual position had come to him in early adolescence in a recurrent dream; the distinct and extraordinary message was this: both God and the Devil had chosen him to be their scribe.

"For," as God Himself, in the form of a great red leather boot, had explained, "the Word is the glue that holds the Universe together. It is what keeps the moon in the sky and the worms in the ground. Without it worms would fly." And shortly after, the Devil had appeared, disguised as a small glass slipper.

"Nothing," the Devil had hissed, "exists until it is seen."

It was then that he bought himself the camera. And at the tender age of fifteen, when other boys are out learning the languages of the flowers and the bees, he spent all his time recording all the sacred substance of existence: random flavors, the exact color and consistency of a stool, galactic calamities, the quantity of sediment clinging to the moist bottom of a cup, fleshy scrapings of all sorts, the shapes and weights of dustballs collected beneath his bed, the position of a spider's web in a sink, maps on the backs of turtles sleeping beneath fountains, the entire population's shoe size, who had died and who was born, the number of dog turds dropped before a gate, of butterflies dancing above a meadow. He photographed every monument, every face, every stone and every stain.

In time he realized that not only did all this information —like thousands of little pins—hold the Universe in place, it also gave him power. And that is when he became the Exorcist. For when Devilry was at work (he called it Organized Aberration) he knew—he had seen the signs long before the first complaints. The odd mushroom, for example, with its thick, milky collar of lacy flesh and runny-nosed features, foretold the illnesses of cows, the abortions of sows, suicides. He had seen the gutted tree, the assembly of hornets, those circular paths that Disaster traces about its victims before closing in. And recognizing the knots, he knew how to unwind them and so unbind the victim.

For years he was considered the greatest Exorcist of them all; the possessed came from farms and hamlets as far as ninety leagues away to be freed by his spell-breaking. But it did not last, he enjoyed success only to suffer reversal. Simply, he lost touch. The world in all her infinite variousness sprawled out on all fours and he faltered; with growing anguish he knew that he could never get it all down. Not alone. He searched the sky for clues, looked to the migrations of the birds and the planets, but the Universe remained silent, or he had grown deaf.

Men came to him with their sores, their sore hearts, their stories of virgin births and bordello deaths, of bewitched nieces and peaches freezing in July. But he—as lost as a blind man in an unfamiliar alley—could help them no longer; the old formulae rang hollow in the thin air of his dim rooms. Locking his door, he crept to his attic hoard of notebooks, glass negatives and sepia images for comfort, and perhaps inspiration, to discover that all had been overturned and smashed by rats, corrupted by mites and rain. He knew then that he had an enemy. And his enemy was Time.

He thought over his previous failures. The fresh headstone photographed only to be defaced by a passing bird (he had taken a new photograph and then it had rained), a garden rendered unrecognizable by a mole, a roof by a hurricane—and so it had hit him at last: his photographs, his careful notes did not belong to him, but to Time. Time was Master. And if the seconds marched forward with inspiring regularity, on the sidelines everything was in mad disorder: a rowdy drooling from balconies, a stampeding of innocents underfoot, the loss of hats and tempers. Why a bird-dropping there, in that very corner, at that very moment? And just after he, the Chosen Scribe, had done his work? Was he being tested? Was he somebody's fool?

The Exorcist tramps through the woods painfully aware of infinitely numerous rustlings and buzzings, the unfathomable quantities of leaves, of moldering debris, of seeds. And then, as he defecates behind a tree, he cries out, with all the passion of discovery:

"The Universe is movement! Time is everything!" And if he, the Exorcist, wants to regain control of the country that is quickly slipping from his grasp (people are talking; witches are infiltrating the landscape and he has been unable to shake them—nails in urine have not worked, the usual incantations in pigsties, nor the braying at dawn beneath a donkey skin beside a virgin's bed), he will have to deal with the Devil alone. For does not this all prove that the pie is unevenly sliced? That Time does not belong to Eternity, the Evermore of Goodness, God's sluggish country of Pure Lead, but to the pie's black backside? Time belongs to the Devil!

As he walks home he realizes why for years he has been fascinated by excrement—his own and that of others, human and animal. (Long ago he had conceived a plan to photograph the village population's every elimination and had plotted of public places equipped with cameras. This had been forgotten when he had become obsessed with moulting insects—Time again! That provocative shedding of skins!)

"Freedom," he wheezes, "is a myth of the mind, a sickness unto disorder." Forgetting to remove his shoes, he climbs into bed and waits for signs.

"There is no free will in Eternity," he mutters, pulling the covers up over his head, "on the dark side of the pie there are no choices. And on the luminous side there is nothing to choose!" As he dozes, a bright glass slipper spins in the void above his head. He recognizes it at once:

"O Beelzebub!" he cries. "Give me the flaming key to your sacred room! Make me your High-Appointed Peeping Tom!" For answer, the shifting stuff of fancy flits before him like the stained and agitated bodies of simple animals seeping their lives out beneath a lens. He sees the planets stuck like sequins to the shell of limbo, pierced to facilitate the migrations of the dead; he perceives that the edge of the world is as sharp as a knife, that those who wander too close have their feet grated like cheese before they are sucked into the mouth of Hell. At dawn he rises and, haunting bushes, empties nests and stretches nets from trees. Later as the Devil whispers, he probes feathers for clues about eclipses; he slices the livers of lizards to uncover the secrets of stars, and counts the teeth of cats to discover the migrations of rats, the paths of plagues. Returning to bed, the Devil's insinuations hot in his ears, he sinks his teeth into the palpitating sugarplum of Dreamland, and straddling the corpulent finger of sleep, thrusting hard, fucks Time.

He knows now that he will succeed; the Power will be his again, and greater than it ever was. No more vassal of two lords, shipwrecked upon a sea of conflicting evidence, but the Devil's lone Right Hand, he will be King of the thickest slice, that seething and fermenting slice called Life. And as in a dream just before dawn, the ultimate proof that the birth of the marked child is of particular consequence to himself, the infant's guardian has come, pounding on his door, to wake him and to ask for his advice in the *Naming*. And this has never happened before. And indeed, it is the first time that anyone has come to him for help in months.

In his oddly agitated manner, emphasizing certain words and phrases with raised eyebrows and astonishing gesticulations, he speaks just above a whisper and with haste, assuring Edma that she was right to come to him (Divinely Inspired, she corrects him, I dreamt of the Mandrake and knew it must refer to you), that it is not by accident that the child has been born stained (The Devil's own work, Edma agrees, the child's mother was a shameless whore!); that names are guardian spirits, their task to deflect the gravitational pulls of lesser destinies.

"The priest knows nothing of Naming," the Exorcist confides.

"Nor much about anything else!" Edma agrees. "God knows, a man who is satisfied with ill-fitting dentures cannot be trusted as a spiritual leader!" She unwraps the babe and holds it up for him to see.

"Remove the Stain!" she demands, convinced of his power. For he has undeniable magnetism; he is wonderfully tall, and his manner is impressively professorial, with a touch of the wizard and a whiff of the demon. She sees his books leaning in monumental heaps; tortuous alchemical instruments of glass and metal throb and whistle in the shadows. He prods the infant's face with a waxy finger.

"It is like fur!" he breathes. "And inexpressibly pagan!"

"Remove it!" she repeats, certain that if he but blows into her face. . . .

"I will not! It is a *signature!*"

"But whose?"

"My Master's." She stares at him expectantly. Who is his master? Dare she ask?

"Belial . . . Abraxas . . . Miquiztli. . . ."

"Demons!" Edma is both terrified and thrilled.

"Dark Lords for Dark Times. And Places. For if the light dwells in Ether, the material world belongs to Shadow. Once," he feverishly rocks the baby to and fro, "in fact at the very beginning of Time, when the planets had only just been formed, aboriginal man stepped up from the muddy vortex that was the world, and pointing to the moon named it Shell. By shell he meant womb, for in his rudimentary tongue, both words were one, and by *womb*. . . ."

"I beg your pardon!"

"But," he insists, "the infant *is* female? Excuse me, Madame, but if I am to be of assistance. . . ."

"This talk of shells and moons. . . ."

"And wombs, Madame!"

"Aggravating!"

"We should name her Teccuciztecatl. . . ."

"You are mad!" Edma grabs the baby, who begins to wail.

"I said we *should* name her Teccuciztecatl. . . . However, we cannot. This is evident, even to me."

"The mother's name," Edma shouts above the baby's screams, "was Charlotte, and I thought—"

"And the mother's trespass was licentiousness. . . ."

"Exactly! *Licentiousness!*" Edma approves. "She wears the mother's sin, and why not her name? My niece was depraved!" Edma shouts, warming to her subject, "and my sister-in-law was depraved—the branch was rotten to the pulp and the fruit was poison! I warned my brother! Hadn't I seen the way she walked, impudent trollop? Hadn't I seen her laugh? O impudent, impudent, shameless strumpet that she was! And did he listen? Not on your life! Turned a deaf ear! Got what he deserved! A bed of snakes!"

"Charlotte. . . ." He thought it over. "I like the way it fills the mouth."

CHAPTER
4

When the little brass bell jangled and Emile in striped pajamas went to the door, he expected to see the postman with a seed catalogue, or perhaps Père Poupine back from the swamp with a living string of frogs' legs. No one else ever visited the house. But the man who introduced himself as "Ali-Hassan Popa" was a perfect stranger. Dressed in a black astrakhan overcoat, short and pear-shaped, he was very like the drypoint engraving Emile had admired earlier that week in the *Univers Illustré* entitled *The Missing Link*— a fashionable oddity touring the country in a small, tasselled cage on wheels. For he was literally covered with hair. His eyeballs alone were free of the stuff, and as is the rule with many redheaded men his beard—immense and wooly— was very black; indeed it was impossible to tell where his head stopped and his coat began. From the top of his skull a thick orange fringe fell straight to those impressive attachments, his eyebrows. Hair of both colors coiled from his nostrils, sprouted from the tip of his nose and bristled in generous bunches from his ears. The man was a garden and Emile took to him at once. Glowing with vigorous health and bonhomie, Ali-Hassan Popa crossed the threshold and grasping Emile's hand enunciated emphatically:

"Monsieur. Vizir Enterprises has considered 1,001 names. Yours, however, provoked our particular attention. Allah be praised!" And stepping back, and mopping his face with a large, exotic-looking silk handkerchief, he paused to admire Emile, his entire attitude suggesting the successful conclusion to an arduous journey.

Emile blushed, and having offered Ali-Hassan Popa Edma's empty chair, seized upon the occasion to fill to the brim two mustard glasses with wine. Monsieur Popa drank his down thirstily and eagerly accepted another, followed by two more. Emile, relishing a drink so early in the morning and with such unusual company, sipped his wine slowly, holding on to his glass with both hands like a shy boy. One drink more and Popa rose to place the empty bottle and glasses carefully down in Edma's virginal sink. Then sitting down heavily at the far side of the table said:

"Monsieur. I said you have been chosen. You will be wanting to know what it is you have been chosen *for*."

Emile, bending forward expectantly, held his breath. He had seen as soon as Popa had entered that he carried a mysterious black leather box, generously studded with an impressively large gold lock. And now he knew that there was something in there for *him*. And Popa, spreading his palms out before him, as if to warm them by the fire of Emile's radiant face, said:

"My brother, you have been chosen Beneficiary Extraordinary. Beneficiary *of* the Extraordinary." Popa sat back and from sheer excitement Emile giggled.

"Trust," Popa continued. "Trust in me. In this propitious hour." And raising a finger in the air like the Hierophant before his disciple: "And not one word. No questions, please. Above all: *Trust!* And no questions!"

Emile's jaw had dropped and a fine thread of spittle dangled from his lips. It had not occurred to him to doubt this strange, marvelous man! He itched to possess the secret of the black box and with joy knew it was soon going to be revealed to him.

Ali-Hassan Popa is whispering:

"And now, silence. Perfect silence. The silence of the sands, the silence of the dreaming sphinx, the silence of Scheherazade when she is sleeping. . . ." And with the flourish of a prestidigitator, he reaches inside his coat and pulls out a large, soft, midnight-blue cloth and lays it upon the kitchen table, taking care to smooth out what is already perfectly smooth with seductive movements of his two plump hands. Spellbound, Emile does not see that although the man's nails are impeccable, his wrists, sliding out from under his shirt-cuffs, are filthy.

"*Mon ami*. You are about to see something new, so new that the sun has not set upon it! And yet soon it will be as familiar to every household as salt. And, Monsieur, just as indispensable."

"Insensible!" Emile repeats, breathing hard.

"In-di-spensable. Something indispensable for your household, you and your family. You have a family?"

"A w-w-w—"

"A wife! Good! For you and your wife to cherish. Forever." And bowing before Emile he adds: "I am deeply honored—yes, trust that I am deeply honored, dear friend, more than I can say. . . . Silence. This is an important moment."

Emile, mopping his brow, rises from his chair convinced that he is about to receive a medal. Wouldn't it be better if he asked Monsieur Popa to wait for a moment so that he can prepare for this and put on his Sunday suit? But Ali-Hassan Popa says firmly:

"Please sit down. And close your eyes. The moment is at hand."

Emile, pulling on his ear painfully, screws his eyes tightly shut. It is, since his wedding, the gravest moment of his life. He hears a crisp *click*—the box has been opened! Had it contained a certified relic of Jehovah's own fossil brain, he could not be more moved.

"*Now!*"

Emile opens his eyes and, wiping the spittle from his lips, gazes upon the infinite indigo ocean of the kitchen table. In the very center of that majestic sea a thing lies, shining in the sun. He rises from his chair and approaches the table on tiptoe.

"W-W-W-Why it's a b-b-b—"

"A bread knife. Exactly."

"Monsieur. You are confused, and well you might be. But listen! If you are looking at what appears to be an ordinary (if unquestionably a very handsome) bread knife, in point of fact you are seeing a remarkable, a consummate, an *extraordinary* bread knife."

"Ex-Ex-Ex-tra-or-or-ordinary!" Emile bellows. (Truly it is the largest, the shiniest, the sharpest-looking knife that he has ever seen, and his confusion and disappointment wane as quickly as his curiosity waxes.)

"Brother, sit down. This knife is not like any other. It has been made by Vizir Enterprises to last. Not for a day, not for a year, not for fifty years, but for *ever*. It is an ever-sharp knife. An ever-bright knife. Made of metal more precious than silver, platinum or gold. This knife is made of Eternal. Remember that name."

"E-Eternal," Emile whispers. And sitting back, he folds his arms across his chest and smiles, staring expectantly into Popa's warm brown eyes. He has never been so happy.

"Eternal!" he guffaws, slapping his knees.

"Brother," says Popa, picking up the knife and placing it on the table within Emile's reach, "this is but a small part of the whole. Haroun-al-Raschid himself could not crave greater treasure!" And as Emile stares, giddy no more but as solemn as a pillar of petrified salt, Popa picks up the mysterious box and placing it on the table with a very satisfactory *thud,* lifts the lid and a number of little brass hinges. To Emile's infinite delight, the box unfolds like an accordion and he sees, spread out upon that royal field, dozens of gleaming knives—knives of every conceivable shape and size and for every conceivable use, clutched ceremoniously in the grasp of one hundred gold-stitched fingers. These knives have more effect upon Emile's famished imagination than the cyclopean jewel-hoard had upon the sailor Sindbad.

"Eternity. . . ." Emile drools.

"Eternal," Ali-Hassan Popa corrects him. "But yes. They will last an Eternity. And they are yours."

"M-M-M?"

"Yours."

Emile weeps. Ali-Hassan Popa places a pen and a thick document before him.

"Please. I am now asking for my deplacement fee, to be paid in installments. I have come from far—and you were hard to find. Do not misinterpret, the knives are a gift."

But Emile, at once despondent, cries:

"The b-b-b!"

"The bread knife is yours! Just sign here. . . ."

"The b-b-b-! The b-box!! I wa-want the *box!*"

"Ah! I see! *Hélas!*" Popa looks pensive. "I am so sorry! The box is not included! It is, as you have appreciated, a very solid article, handmade of the finest exotic woods, trimmed with Persian cut velvet, genuine gold fixtures, the whole generously upholstered in unusually fine quality baby veal hide. I was planning to throw in the blue cloth. But to give you the box was not Vizir Enterprises' intention."

Emile is stricken. A tear swells in his eye and spills out onto his cheek.

"How m-m-m?"

Ali-Hassan Popa is not an insensitive man. "Well, brother," he says, "I don't know. It's an unusual piece of merchandise. There is none other like it in the world. How much do you have?"

In a flash, Emile is up from his chair. He disappears into the bedroom and reaches into Edma's full laundry bag, pulling out a tight wad of bills. His head bowed, he runs back into the kitchen and slams the cash triumphantly down before the astonished Popa, who looks at the wad with frank admiration. Picking it up, he unrolls and flips through it quickly, moistening his index finger with his tongue.

"Whoredom!" he whispers, forgetting himself. "You've got a small fortune here!"

Emile nods his head wildly and grins. Popa reaches across the table and takes back his pen and his document, and turning it over begins an involved series of calculations.

"Fixtures," he notes aloud, "solid gold. Leather: genuine baby veal. . . . I'll tell you what," he says after a breathtaking moment, sitting back amiably and looking deeply into Emile's eyes: "I *like* you."

"I-I-I like *you!*" Emile admits, blushing furiously.

". . . And I'd like you to keep the box." Emile groans. "Even if it *is* worth a good deal more than what you've got here. Of course," he adds generously, "you're paying cash and I am considering that fact very seriously. Believe me."

"I b-b-believe!" says Emile. The knives gleam in the sun like the enchanted runes of some fabulously ancient and powerful alphabet.

CHAPTER

5

Edma returned home very pleased. The Exorcist had given her a magnet and an amulet of polished brass embellished with the image of the hideous rooster-headed Abraxas, Master of the 365 Aeons, or Emanations of the First Cause. She wore it between her wasted breasts, beside the gold cross that had belonged to her brother and the medal of Saint Fiacre that he had received at First Communion. As the Exorcist had directed, Charlotte was washed in salt water. She was fed from a bladder-shaped stoneware bottle with a brown india-rubber nipple. Edma licked her finger and dipped it in the salt, making the sign of the cross over Charlotte's disfigured face before swaddling her and tucking her into the crib. She then purged the kitchen of the hostile configurations of evil stars and jealous neighbors with the small blue magnet that, spinning from a thread of catgut, filled the room with cleansing vibrations.

That afternoon, Edma went out for fresh bread and the sundry objects that the kitchen-yard creatures and Emile's vegetable patch could not provide. She was held up for thirty minutes at the bakery where Madame Fesse, the baker's saturnine spouse, described with morbid loquacity her recent gallbladder infection and the surgery that had ensued. And those who had had the tact or the time to listen to the bitter end were rewarded with a look at those precious artifacts, Madame Fesse's lugubrious gallstones;

not as spectacular as a glimpse of baby Charlotte's unwholesome face, or the curious vision of the Téton twins, but the ladies grudgingly admitted to themselves that La Fesse's stones were well worth seeing.

"Often they are wonderfully colorful!" Madame Fesse exclaimed breathlessly, displaying in her moist palm three brown lumps like bits of old chocolate retrieved on laundry day from a schoolboy's soiled pocket.

"The doctor showed me some that I could have sworn were gold!"

It was apparent to everyone that the doctor's archaeological forays into Madame Fesse's anatomy had had a most salubrious effect upon the lady's habitually despondent nature. She was positively radiant, her sallow cheeks rosy; she had recently dyed her hair strawberry blonde and her blouse, stretched tightly across her breasts, was clean and ironed.

"It is offensive," said Edma after, "the pride with which she displays for the price of a loaf of bread the questionable refuse of her objectionable tripes! I hear that any person unfortunate enough to indulge in a lemon pie may peek at that breast tumor she had removed last January. They say she keeps it in a jar in the cupboard along with the almond butter. The woman lacks taste and she lacks humility."

This was said to the greengroceress, a robust Swiss whose breasts, as lavish as La Fesse's, concealed an equally generous heart.

"Ah," she said in her lilting accent, "she does no harm."

"She will pay for the Sin of Pride," Edma replied firmly. "The Devil has seen those stones of hers and that odious jar, and whatever other filth she cleaves to! Much good all that garbage will do her on Judgment Day!"

"Heavens! You *are* severe!"

"As is God," Edma replied. "How's the cheese?"

"It is very fine cheese, Madame."

"Well then, cut me a slice, not too thick and from the inside. I do not intend to pay for any stale crusts. Righteous individuals do not expose their peculiarities to all and sundry as if they were objects of piety."

Edma took her parcel, and angry with La Fesse, the greengroceress and even the piece of cheese (for which she feared she had paid too dearly), left the shop frowning. She was still frowning when she arrived home. She found Charlotte soaked in urine and shrieking in her cradle. Emile had left her to tend to his cabbages and Brussels sprouts, and had tarried absentmindedly.

Edma jammed a wad of soft bread into Charlotte's open mouth to shut her up. She then changed her and prepared the gruel which Charlotte, half choked, could not swallow. Edma grabbed her by the feet to smack her vigorously upon the back, but once the piece of bread had been knocked from her esophagus Charlotte was so enraged and terrified that she screamed for an hour. Her temper is as ugly as her face, Edma decided, but she knew enough to rock the baby until tears and hiccups subsided and she was able to drink from the cold stoneware bottle.

CHAPTER

6

After their habitual late-afternoon coffee, Edma, having be-
wildered Emile with a tangled history of gallstones, moons
and magnets, went into the bedroom to fetch her laundry and
discovered that her life savings were no longer there. Her
hands to her face she raced back to the kitchen and howled:

"Emile! My nest egg! It's gone!"

"G-G-Gone," Emile agreed.

"Who has *dared?*" she bellowed, ready for murder.
"Before God I swear," she added, looking intently at the
ceiling, with such intensity in fact that her eyes seemed to
pierce it, the attic roof and the heart of Cosmic Law Itself,
"I will have him *destroyed!*" Emile cringed against the sink
in terror.

"It was here this morning," she continued, "it was stolen
while I was gone."

"Gone," Emile whispered.

"But who? *Who* came while I was gone?"

"P-P-P!" Emile spluttered, totally undone.

Edma knew it was not the postman who had obediently
delivered seed catalogues twice a year for twenty-two years
and who wore an immaculate uniform besides. It could
only be:

"*Poupine!*"

"Poupine?" marveled Emile, seizing upon this straw as
might a drowning man.

Père Poupine, the professional vagrant and inspired drunk, was small and wiry, his mouth fine and quick to grin. He and his mongrel Fleas survived by catching and selling frogs, snails and crawfish. Occasionally Fleas' sensitive proboscis would lead them to a cluster of rare *Boletus appendiculatus* and thereafter both man and dog would drink themselves into insensibility.

On Saturday afternoons after the lottery returns had come in, Père Poupine would entertain his pals in the following manner: he would first blow smoke through his ears; he would then imitate, and with unquestionable talent, the sexual ditties of frogs, crickets and cows; and finally he would fart—and in perfect harmony—the popular tunes of the day, invariably concluding with two favorites of his own invention, "She Made a Good Cassoulet" and "The Wayward Nun."

She wore an ample wimple
It hid her dimpled chin,
She wore an ample mantle
It kept her safe from sin . . .

His real name, Archange Poupin, had long been forgotten, and the nickname, Poupine, an inevitable invention of the local brats, had stuck to him like a hungry tick. Translated loosely it means cocklice—an epithet in fact unjust. Poupine was grimy and he made bad smells, but he was not lousy. And this, considering how he lived, was an accomplishment.

All that week Poupine had spent his nights beneath a persistent drizzle harvesting edible snails with the help of a green kerosene lamp and a large wire basket. And that morning he had brought several thousand *petit-gris* to Madame Saignée's café-restaurant in exchange for a week's soup and insobriety. He was already soused when Edma burst into the café. Those cronies still conscious fell silent, forgetting their games of dominoes to watch with astonishment and glee her apocalyptic appearance. Only Madame Saignée, true to her habitual waxen attitude of restrained hysteria, remained unmoved.

Edma saw Poupine at once, excreting a faint radiance in a grim corner of the dim café; it occurred to her that very conceivably a match struck in his vicinity would cause him to ignite. And she would have thought the punishment just.

"*Poupine!*" she roared, the gristle on her severely buttoned chest in Vesuvian upheaval, "*you filthy thief!*"

"Hé, Hé, Hé!" cried a gnomish drunk from under a wool cap that was far too large for him. "My pal's filthy, maybe, but he's no filthy thief!"

Edma boomed: "He's stolen my nest egg! He's drinking it now!"

Poupine, Fleas comatose at his feet, perceived Edma through the shifting mists of his intemperance, scratched his thorny jowl thoughtfully and mumbled:

"What is she chattering about?" And looking to his friends for assistance called out: "What the hell's a nest egg?"

"Ah *Diable!*" Edma cried as she grabbed him by his collar, which was so worn it tore off in her fist. He flailed at her with arms that were numb and loosely strung and fell from his chair to the floor with a soggy thud. And as the men hissed and booed, Edma dragged Poupine like a sack of groats to the door and heaved him into the street where the bright light of the setting sun hit him in the face like a basin of nitric acid. Painfully he pulled himself to his feet.

"*Fille de garce.*" He stood oscillating and blinking. With her bonnet, Edma swatted him into activity.

"Ouch!" he yelped. "Gently, lady! Where the hell we going?"

"To the *Gendarmerie!*" she shouted, still slapping away at his head and legs. "I am having you arrested!"

35

Poupine vaguely supposed that he was guilty of something, but of what?

By now all his cronies had tumbled, cursing and spitting, out into the street after him.

"Show her your broom!" roared the dwarf. "Her chimney needs sweeping!"

"By my prunes!" Poupine replied. "Heresh one shimney should be condemned!"

As Edma and Poupine entered the *Gendarmerie,* the men pissed into the street and produced a savant variety of catcalls and further advice:

"Melt her cheese, Poupine!"

"Give her old fish a taste of your anchovy!" And so on.

Once inside, Edma insisted that Poupine strip:

"He took my nest egg this morning," she explained to the *Brigadier,* and with unveiled menace showed her sparse teeth, "and he's been at the café drinking it up all day. I'd swear to God it's still on him!"

The *Brigadier* was perplexed. In his seedy way, Archange Poupin was one of La Folie's quieter citizens.

First Poupine removed his shoes.

"Pestilential hell!" cried Edma. Then he removed his trousers. "Father in Heaven, he's not wearing drawers!" Edma threw her skirts over her face, disclosing thereby her own intimate and voluminous garment split down the middle.

Père Poupine spent one night in jail (where his left ear was bitten off by a rat); and once the *Brigadier* (after a visit to Madame Saignée, Poupine's witness) had convinced Edma to drop charges, he was set free. The evening of his release, looking the War Hero with his generously bandaged head, Poupine diverted his pals with the following banter:

"Compeers (an' the *Brigadier* hisself will vouchsafe for my verarse-ity), when Edma got it into her head she must see my bare bum an' upon seein' it were moved to throw her petticoats un-arse-isted over her calamitous Arse-yrian phiz (*sacré centmille de bon Dieu!*) I swear to God that I did see (an' unwillin'ly I arse-ures you!) her nest which (as she said herself an' as we'd all arse-umed) was empty. And (may God strike me down as I stand if I lie) I did also see, sure as I see you, that (by its arse-uredly grim arse-pect) this was a nest from which there had never been nothing to steal. . . ."

> *. . . No more young, she was not old*
> *But round and ripe and fruity;*
> *She had a great big frying pan—*
> *Big enough for any man and O!*
> *She made a fine cassoulet! Ohé!*
> *She made a good cassoulet!*
>
> *Young no more but not so bad*
> *In fact the best I've ever had—*
> *She had a great black cooking pot*
> *And I can tell you it was hot! O!*
> *She had a nice casserole! Ohé!*
> *She made a good cassoulet!*

CHAPTER
7

Aunt Edma's yard, like a medieval forest, afforded little pleasure and much to fear. The charming, furry rabbits, munching comfortably in their greenwire hutches, were lascivious creatures given over entirely to the dubious delights of fornication. It was impressed upon Charlotte that the rabbits were diseased, that at any moment their ears would fall off, that this malady was highly communicable. Charlotte, limping about painfully in tightly buttoned boots, must not go near the chickens either, for fear they fly into her face and peck out her eyes, mistaking them for grubs. Aunt Edma had explained (as best as she could to a small child) that if the chickens' eggs were blessed gifts of the Lord God to whom Charlotte must be eternally grateful (what could be more perfect than the egg, complete unto itself as a pure soul nesting in Heavenly Embrace—entire and clean of sin, smooth without and within, sealed with all the mystery of a reliquary), the fowl themselves were tainted, absurd creatures held fast in the merciless grasp of greed.

> *To be perfect as an egg,*
> *Perfect people must be dead.*
> (Charlotte)

Often as she sat on the back steps at a safe distance, her hands folded demurely in her lap, watching the chickens scrabbling in the compost and the rabbits stirring in their straw, Charlotte's heart would be seized and, like a chick within a fist, flutter and still. When with a dull thump it resumed its normal rhythm, she suffered an acute sense of loss. For those instants of panic—like the bright flames of God's Word—illuminated her tedious life.

School was a disaster that lasted seven minutes. The moment she stepped into the courtyard an older boy, dim and dirty, damned with the skull of pithecanthropus, his naked calves and thighs ravaged with the bites of fleas, pelted her with clumps of dry mud. "Evil Eye!" he boomed, lumbering after when she ran to the center of the yard to stand with her back to an ancient linden tree. She was at once surrounded by her peers, a snot-nosed swarm of battered peasant brats who, when not stanching bloody noses with their sleeves in the corners of murky kitchens, were weeping themselves to sleep in the terrifying stink of the pigpen paying the stiff penalties of crimes real and imagined. A boy Charlotte's age, with the pinched face of a ferret and the ferret's sharp teeth and shifty look, was the first to throw a shoe. Charlotte slipped to the ground, pulled her knees to her chest and hid her face in her hands. Evil Eye! Evil Eye! Evil Eye! It was a game, they circled the tree holding hands, skipping together. Evil Eye! Evil Eye! Evil Eye! Charlotte felt the Stain twitching beneath her hand. She was kicked in the shins and then it rained pebbles, pen-nibs and slates. Just after she was hit in the head with an open bottle of ink—

> . . . *That impotent, timorous pinhead*
> *That duck with a horn on his beak,*
> *That ludicrous hack, Master Quack! Quack! Quack!*
> (Poupine)

the schoolmaster appeared from the classroom where he had been praying God for the courage he needed to face yet another year. With his fop's lisp (for which the brats had dubbed him The Spits, Split Lips, The Shits, Split Ends and Master Spits) he scolded them as harshly as he could in the midst of stampede and uproar and, kicking his way to Charlotte, grabbed her by the elbow and rushed her home. As they ran from the gate and into the street, a desk and a bench crashed into the courtyard, followed by a flight of books. Charlotte heard someone shout for matches. Her face was smeared with ink and with tears.

Edma stood on the threshold and listened with a grim expression as Master Spits—who was screaming—suggested a private tutor for Charlotte and a veil. But Edma said: It is God's wish that the mother's sin be read upon the face of the child.

After lunch, Charlotte took a nap. The Stain was warm beneath her hand. Feeling its familiar shape, its softness and heat, she closed her eyes and smiled. For it had occurred to her that the Stain was more than the emblem of her mother's mysterious trespass; it was a mark that God Himself had laid upon her to set her apart from the cruel, snot-nosed creatures who went to school!

Thus it was Emile who taught Charlotte how to read. As Edma boiled the Saturday wash over a slow fire out in the kitchen yard, the smell of homemade soap sharpening the air, Emile and Charlotte pored over Emile's seed catalogues together. Soon they were so well-thumbed the pages were soft and wrinkled, the texture of old lettuce. Miraculously the words corresponded to pictures:

"L-l-look! Cha-Charrle. . . . A t-t-tulip! *T-tulip!*"

"Tulip," Charlotte repeated, carefully inscribing it on a squared piece of brown wrapping paper.

One evening before supper, Emile took her to the greengrocery where they bought a school notebook with lined pages, some white drawing paper in a large canary-yellow envelope and a box of pastels. Edma scolded Emile for the expense, but she allowed Charlotte to keep everything. That night Charlotte drew the sumptuous bird of paradise tulip. Emile said that it looked a-a-alive.

The seed catalogues were the only books in the house apart from the Bible, a pamphlet from Lourdes about Bernadette Soubirous, and a cookery book which contained lurid diagrams demonstrating how to bleed, gut and truss fowl. Emile insisted that his catalogues contained e-everything a p-p-person n-need kn-know. Indeed, they contained astrological information, weather forecasts and even nature stories. Charlotte's favorite:

Death of the Robin

Death reaches into the tallest trees. As best he can the little robin hides within the leaves, but no hideaway is safe from Death! The darling innocent falls ill, his feathers droop. Trembling he perches with silent beak tucked beneath tarnished wing, his eyes screwed shut as if the sun would scorch them. For hours on end he stoops thus upon the branch. From time to time a weak twitter escapes from his parched beak. . . . Suddenly he is seized with a convulsive fit, his feathers bristle and his claws—the nails of which have hideously lengthened—open and he falls from the tree to hit the earth like a ball of lead.

"Just like corpses!" Charlotte had been reading aloud. "Just like corpses!" Edma repeated, knitting. "Their nails grow in the grave!"

Emile and Charlotte also counted together. On page 16 of the Vilmorin Spring Catalogue, 1880, Charlotte counted six sorts of tomato:

Break of day, Cherry. Earliana, Ficcaraji, Marmande, Scarlet Dream.

But on the following page, the tomatoes, like the robin, were dying.

"M-mildew!" Emile pointed to the terrible word. "M-Mildew of the T-To-mato!"

Bronze spotted wilt. Emile's eyes filled with tears. He caressed the image of the sick tomato with his hand. On a clean sheet of paper Charlotte wrote:

Disease
Spotted wilt

The infected leaves roll up. Open, running sores infect the stem. She wrote the words

Pustule
Destructive Phoma

The tomatoes looked like warts. "They look like La Fesse's tumor." (Edma.)

Burn the infected plants. (Vilmorin.)

There were pictures of turtles and tritons. Tritons were useful. A gardener was joyful when he saw one.

Tritons eat snails and they eat slimes. They also eat one another. (Edma.)

Charlotte copied the drawings of the sick tomatoes, the curious nodosities poisoning the roots, the gaping wounds of pustular plants, their curled leaves. She drew Prodigious Peas and Sugar Peas. The Early Radish. Healthy and unhealthy strawberries. If only she could have a turtle to keep in the garden! She would name it Jesus Christ. But Edma said: Turtles, like all reptiles, are evil.

Once Charlotte had mastered the seed catalogues:

cauliflower
mé tal dé hyde
rhubarb

she read the pamphlet devoted to Bernadette Soubirous—
the miraculous grotto, the water and watercress she had
found, and her spectacular visions of the Virgin Mary. God
is in my heart, Bernadette was fond of saying, my heart
falters with love.

Charlotte had no toys: Extravagance and vanity! Vanity and
waste! (Edma.) With her pastels she drew faces on the
smooth pebbles Emile had laid down years before in the
garden path. She gave them names and personalities, and
acted out the life of Jesus. His Wonderful Birth and Horrendous End. Every day, with harsh screeches very much
like Edma's own, God scolded baby Jesus into humble
submission. But Mary—a small, sad face, yellow hair and
a ruff—was kind, and once her baby was chastised, she invented lullabies to soothe Him to sleep. Jesus, Charlotte
said, dreams of starlight. And indeed, Jesus, in a medicine
box, beamed. Jesus, Charlotte said, turning Him over, is
having a nightmare. His Father is watching Him bleed to
death!
    Joseph, like Emile, was a stutterer and did not do or say
much. He had sheep to look after and a magic garden in
which the fruit and vegetables, arranged in a maze, had
faces. Jesus did not eat these vegetables but took His
nourishment directly from the sun. Facing south He baked
like a little loaf all afternoon in a chink which the rain had
licked out of the stone wall. From time to time Charlotte
would take Him into her hand to feel His warmth. God-

the-Father was a bodiless voice until Charlotte was inspired to talk into one of Emile's pails, imparting His Word with a most satisfactory, hollow eeriness. Thereafter the pail, turned over upon the ground, stood in for Him (as well as for His Church, for He was quite large enough to hold all the pebbles within Himself, and was used, perhaps irreverently, to bring everyone into the garden shed each evening, so that they should not lose their faces in the rain).

The pebble-people, animals, vegetables and fish, could often be seen parading together in sinuous lines made festive with empty seed packets stuck into the earth on sticks like flags. Jesus sat in His box, Mary on a scrap of black bombazine, and Joseph on a leaf. The plain pebbles of the path—a devout and expressionless multitude—were brushed aside to make room for the Holy Family. One day Joseph was accidentally kicked into a flat stone designated as the Pope. God-the-Father punished this perversity by dropping Joseph down the well—a punishment so awesome that Charlotte was riddled with guilt for days. God, standing stolidly upside-down at the end of the path, looked dreadfully ominous. It took all the courage she could muster to remove Him to the shed and cover Him with rags so that He could no longer be witness to what she was doing. Yet, even when blinded and banished to a sunless corner, He continued to exert a weird influence. Whenever she thought of Him, a monstrous wing would blot out the sky.

CHAPTER

8

Edma and Emile kept to themselves. But for the Exorcist, who visited often—prodding Charlotte's liver and ribs, measuring and photographing the Stain and giving her powders to drink or inhale from odd, indigo-blue bottles and sickly green boxes decorated with pyramids and snakes —they received no visitors. Edma was forever at war with the neighbors; she had made enemies of them for life by poisoning their domestic animals which she despised for fornicating and defecating in public, in the street, without shame. The only time Charlotte saw other people was on rare visits to the greengroceress and when Edma took her to church.

They went to church every Sunday and on Holy Days and whenever there was a funeral. Babies, particularly the newborn, died with far greater frequency than old people. The wee coffins, draped in embroidered white satin and decorated with pearls and silver thread, were the most sumptuous objects that she was ever to see. Once they witnessed a wedding. The bride's *coiffe* was black because, as Edma explained, her hazelnut was smashed. The meaning of this was obscure.

"Her hazelnut, Aunt?"

"She is spoiled! Soiled!"

Charlotte looked the bride over. Her dress and apron, her belt and ribbons, even her shoes, were impeccably clean. She must be soiled within, Charlotte decided. Perhaps the bride had eaten filthy food for lunch?

"Did she eat tripes for lunch, Aunt?" Charlotte tugged at Edma's sleeve.

"Speak only when you've something sensible to say!"

That night Charlotte prayed to the Lord God, the God of the Tulip and the Tomato, the God of the Strawberry and the Scarlet Gem, to be invited to a wedding. And clearly He heard, for not long after a young man appeared at the door with small bouquets of bud roses pinned to his shirt and an invitation to the wedding feast of Bébert Prouteau, son of Edma's cousin Nestor. As he explained, he was Bébert's best man, and the wedding feast would take place the following Saturday afternoon at Prouteau's farm. The recently orphaned bride would be moving in directly to live with her in-laws. She was not swollen, and brought with her a dowry of new and used linen.

Charlotte wondered about the not swollen. She supposed that he meant the bride was very thin, one of those wonderful persons who can pass through the eye of a needle. How she would love to be that thin!

"Oh, *Aunt!*" she breathed, clinging to Edma's stiff apron. "Please?"

But Edma pushed her aside with her foot and pretended not to know who the young man was talking about—for Nestor had been remembered in her brother's will, and Edma had put up a furious battle, insisting that everything was hers. And although the land he inherited was little compared to all that she received—vineyards, orchards, pasture land and a dairy (the rent from which enabled her to live with Emile and Charlotte very comfortably)—she had not seen Nestor Prouteau for years. When the young man insisted, Edma wrung her hands together and complained in a steady, grating whine that Prouteau's farm, "Trou au Loup," was a good seven kilometers from La

Folie, that a wolf had been sighted in the woods, that they would have to spend the night, that she had nothing to wear, that her health was poor, that on such an occasion a goose would be expected of her and would have to be carried all that tedious way and so forth and so on. Charlotte was mortified, but Emile proposed that the kind young man could "c–c–c–carry the g-goose."

To Charlotte's delight, Edma agreed. She was curious and Prouteau, after all, was family. Perhaps his conscience had been bothering him. Perhaps he intended to give the "stolen" land back? And so the young man was invited in, given a small glass of sweet wine and a slice of cold pie; soon he set off with yet another bouquet pinned at his breast and the goose—its neck broken—tucked beneath his arm. Charlotte was not allowed to wave good-bye from the front door, and so she ran up the stairs to her room hoping to see him from her window. Opening it wide with a clatter that brought Edma running, she called out after him "Good-bye! Good-bye!" and when he turned, "Thank you! O! Thank you!"

"Impertinent trollop!" Edma shouted, running into the room. And she slapped Charlotte across the mouth.

It was a hot day in June and all the way to the wedding feast, Edma—in a heavy dress of black bombazine and a black bombazine shawl—fretted about the heat, her martyred feet, the insects in the air and the dust in the road. She slapped Charlotte when she walked too quickly and again when she lagged behind. She shook her silly for walking with her toes turned in. Time and time again they had to stop so that Edma could catch her breath, wipe the dust from her face with Emile's best handkerchief and drink blessed water from a tepid bottle. She complained that Emile's suit was shiny in the seat, that he had neglected to trim the unseemly hair that was protruding from his ears.

She grieved over her own dress—it was too tight at the throat, it was discolored, she should have worn the new one—had it only been finished in time! But no! She never had time for herself, never, never, never! So busy was she from dawn to dusk, from dawn to dusk, looking after a fool and a freak! Emile, taking this all to heart, stumbled along in the ditch blinking back his tears like a brave, small boy. Charlotte took his hand.

"That's right!" Edma whined. "Always sticking together! Freaks and fools always do!"

At last, to the strident hum of sexually mature insects, they crossed the little bridge that led to Trou au Loup and there, to turn the day into a complete disaster, who did they see sitting on a stool, a pail of frogs propped between his knees, his lips stained purple with wine, cracking ribald jokes—how wet the frogs, how slippery, water friggers he called them—who if not Père Poupine, the poacher, the drunk, the scoundrel, the Nest Egg Thief Himself! Edma let out a hoot of indignation and as swift as a pair of sharp scissors in silk marched to the outhouse and locked herself in. She was certain Poupine had been invited to humiliate her.

Cousin Nestor tried to reason with her, at first politely. He stood at the outhouse door pleading. His guests and family gathered together and watched.

"Edma! Please come out! This is a terrible misunder-standing! Edma!" he begged, "we haven't seen one another for years! The children have grown! My son is a fine young man! The bride wants to meet you! Please come out! Let us celebrate together!"

"I should have known it was a trick!" Edma shouted nasally (for she was holding her nose). "You've always been a trickster, Nestor! A trickster and a cheat!"

Nestor was furious. "That land came to me legally, Edma! Your brother knew I would work it with my own hands. Not rent it out to strangers—play at Kings and Queens!"

"The Queen spits on you!" Edma spat. "I spit on thieves and poachers! Phtoo! Phtoo! Phtoo!"

"Well then, stay where you are!" Nestor shouted, purple with rage. "If you prefer to sit over shit than at table!"

And that is just what Edma did, despite the stench, the flies, the scatological cracks shouted in her direction, the bride's tears, Emile's desperate whimperings, despite the exasperated rattlings and poundings of guests in need. Edma remained barricaded in the outhouse, as fixed as a monument, at war with the entire Universe. As it was impossible to eject her from the privy, Charlotte and Emile joined the others in the house.

The dining room had been decorated in the style known as *Paradis*. The old, saltpetered walls were masked with white linen bed sheets upon which satin ribbons, fresh lilies, white roses and a pair of starched woman's drawers had been pinned. The wedding gifts were heaped together in a corner on the floor: a faience chamberpot with a blue, luxuriously lashed eye painted on the bottom, a wicker baby basket, bellows, a pink pottery bank in the shape of a cow's udder, a cheese mold, a mousetrap, a butter churn, a broom and the bride's gift to the groom—a faience comb box painted with his initials and the feminine genitals framed in red roses—and the groom's gift to the bride—a thick, iron fire-poker with a decorative handle. Père Poupine, his job done, had left, taking with him a roast chicken, a pie and a bottle; but still Edma refused to budge, sticking, as Nestor said she was, to her principles.

Two long oak tables had been put together to make room for the guests—twenty, including Charlotte and two very small children who greedily swilled at their mother's swollen tits, sucking with great pop-popping noises and shamelessly smacking their lips. The tables took up so much room that once everyone was seated it was impossible to get up again without disturbing someone; food brought in from the kitchen was passed around the table from hand to hand.

The bride was a small, giddy creature with greasy skin and a bulbous nose that she shared with at least five other faces in the room. She was wearing a generous helping of lace with which her stubby, red fingers fussed continuously. Her nails had been bitten to the quick and throughout the meal she stole furtive nibbles of cuticle. And now, dinner nearly over, she toyed with a clot of cream, all that remained of the *pièce montée,* a construction one meter high of puff pastry balls filled with whipped cream and stuck together with burnt sugar. The groom was told to leave the room. Cousin Nestor, amid cheers and applause and much energetic clomping of clogged feet, lifted the bride to the table top where she stood, her cheeks blazing, giggling behind her bleeding fingers and twisting this way and that. Charlotte saw her wooden wedding shoes, carved with hazelnuts and leaves. The hazelnut *meant* something, but what? She turned to Emile to ask him and saw that the wine had taken effect and he had fallen asleep, his head propped up on one hand, his mouth wide open. A string of saliva had caught in the bristles of his chin. But then her attention was won by the seamstress, "La Rouge" as she was called— less for the color of her hair (which was blonde) than for the looseness implied by her trade—who reached under the bride's dress (of her own manufacture) and pulled away the garter—a handful of silk ribbons and starched cotton roses. To cheers and loud laughter she held it high above her head and—hand on hip—stamped around her chair like a Spanish dancer. The garter was then tossed back and forth across the table and as the bride stood doubled over with laughter, the women admired it, the men played with it, kissing it, blowing on it, ruffling it with their fingers or nestling it coyly between their thighs, or putting it on their head like a hat, until La Rouge, feigning anger, grabbed it back and wagging it in the air cried above the uproar:

"What will you give me? Who will open the bids?" The bride could not contain herself and shook with a fit of the giggles, jamming her fist into her mouth.

"Ten sous!" offered the best man. "Make it twelve!"

"Twelve sous!" La Rouge was indignant. "Twelve sous isn't nearly enough!" And with a slap on the bride's rump and a twist of her own wrist, La Rouge delineated the bride's curves.

"Bah!" It was the bride's uncle, a burly peasant with a receding hairline and a purple version of the bride's nose. It was his role to bring the price of the garter down. "She's a regular jug-head," he cried. "When she was a brat pissing in rags they hung her by those big ears along with the socks and the smocks to keep her dry! Besides, she's not what I'd call a spring radish!"

There was merry laughter at this; the men slapped their thighs and the women guffawed, although some poked their husbands in the ribs, scolding. For the bride's laughter had ebbed and what was left of her smile was crooked. La Rouge hoisted up her bright taffeta skirts and clambered onto the table, kicking over a glass and stepping into Charlotte's plate. Charlotte saw that she wore an elegant pair of satin shoes with a little heel. Someone hooted:

"Thirteen sous! Not over thirteen!"

"Look at her eyelashes!" cooed La Rouge. "Look at her hair!" And she unpinned the *coiffe* that held the hair in place. Auburn curls spilled over the bride's shoulders, bosom and down her back, transforming her from something dowdy into something sexual, provocative. Her mother-in-law clucked in dismay, pretending to be shocked; the men applauded.

"Fifteen sous!"

"Twenty! Make it a franc."

"Forty sous!"

"It's not real!" The bride's uncle cut in. But La Rouge gave it a tug that caused the girl to cry out.

"It's real!" she shouted triumphantly.

"Hold on," he insisted. "I swear, friends—she's bow-legged!"

"Let's see her legs!" This from the table's far end. "Let's see her ankles and knees!"

"Show them your legs, Joujou!" La Rouge coaxed. "Come on, dearie! Show them how nicely made your legs are!" The bride's lips were trembling and Charlotte could see that she was trying not to cry. Gingerly she lifted her skirts to show off two very hairy ankles.

"Elephantiasis!" he screamed. "Didn't I tell you! It runs in the family. All the women have legs like that, and the men all have *trunks* like elephants!" For an instant he fiddled with his fly. On a dare he was prepared to lay it out upon the table. Instead, he thrust his hand up the bride's skirts and pinched her calves. She yelped and collapsed into tears. La Rouge gathered her up in her arms.

"These are real tears!" she said. "What will you give me for real tears?" And she dangled the garter drolly behind the bride's back.

"Sixty sous!"

"Eighty!"

"One hundred!"

"One hundred sous an' a chicken!"

"I give up!" the uncle bellowed in mock disgust. "Those aren't teats in her bodice, they're peeled onions! The girl's taking you for a ride!"

"And soon she'll be taking the groom for a ride!"

"Five francs it is—and one chicken!" La Rouge tossed the garter to the highest bidder—who was also the drunkest —and the sobbing bride was lifted from the table by the man who had so blissfully abused her, and rocked, as she blubbered, in his embrace.

"There, there, it was all a joke!" he soothed, stroking her hair with his right hand and rubbing between her thighs with his left.

"If she cries now," tittered La Rouge, handing the thick silver coin over to La Tatette, who had been hired to do the laundry, "she'll cry less later!"

The groom was then allowed in and soon he and the bride were kissing; he was panting—he had never before seen her hair unpinned. An enormous tart was sliced, the champagne poured, foaming, into each crystal glass and boisterously consumed. Everyone sang his favorite song at least twice. Edma, who could bear the suffocating stink of the privy no longer, skulked in, occasioning an explosion of amused belches. She sat stiffly in her chair and if she refused to speak, she did accept her share of dessert and a sip of wine. At midnight the bride and groom retired. Sometime during the night the bridal chamber was broken into and the couple forced to drink a "fortifying broth." Guests were sleeping in their chairs and on the floor; because of the wolf-fear, no one dared go home. Indeed, a great she-wolf, apparently rabid, who walked on her hind legs and whistled "like a locomotive," had been seen in the woods near Prouteau's farm—a yellow wolf standing a full two meters high. *Two meters high!* Charlotte shuddered.

Charlotte fell asleep in her chair, her head in Emile's lap. She dreamed of yellow wolves. She dreamed of brides. At dawn she awoke to see the nuptial sheet, stained with dark, brown blood, carried in triumphantly by La Rouge. At once Charlotte imagined that the wolf, disguised as Red Riding Hood, had entered into the bride's window and had climbed into bed with her.

"Has she been eaten? Has she been eaten?" Charlotte ran to Edma, for Emile was still fast asleep and snoring quietly to himself.

"Who? What nonsense is she talking now! How she tries my temper!"

"The *bride!*" Charlotte was sobbing. The sheet was held so that everyone could touch the blood. It would protect them from the stings of hornets and bees for a full twelve months. Without warning, Edma grabbed Charlotte by her hair and forced her face into the sheet for luck, scrubbing the Stain with the bride's fresh blood. Charlotte's screams awoke the entire house, even the newly wedded couple came running; she nearly choked to death on the full glass of red wine that was forced down her throat to calm her. She was so ill that Nestor had to drive her, along with Edma and Emile, back to La Folie in his cow cart.

"Just like her mother!" Edma complained to Nestor. "Impudent scallywag! Always causing trouble!"

CHAPTER

9

Look carefully at the freshly disturbed soil and you will see shining in the sun a derelict rib. The scattered remains of persons deceased are revealed after thaws and heavy rains. Here little Charlotte will accumulate a singular set of ivory pawns: vertebrae, lunates, phalanges and molars.

Charlotte is seven years old. As is usual, her birthday is celebrated by a trip to the cemetery. Charlotte, in black wool coat and stockings, a black ribbon tied to her hair, is wedged between her aunt and uncle for a morning of prayer. The late October sun is hot and the air heavy with the brute stench of boxwood.

As Edma prays and Emile dozes, Charlotte explores the cemetery with her immense grey-green eyes (changeling eyes, Edma calls them, neither here nor there). She observes that the ornate mausoleum squatting ponderously to the left of her mother's grave has a broken step that has slipped to reveal an inky crevice. And this crevice crawls with flies. The mausoleum's stained and pitted frontage is also alive with flies, swarming multitudes clinging to the defunct family's name like grapes. With a thrill, Charlotte recognizes the letters and reads the stones. And it is here, in the cemetery, that she will have her first lesson in geometry:

> *God's love is a circle*
> *Our Hearts sleep within*
> *Safe from Sin.*

and:

The triangle is perfect purity—
God, His Son, the Holy Ghost—
The Blessed Trinity.

Charlotte sees that the triangle itself stirs restlessly beneath a shifting swarm of flies.

She wonders about the grinning cavity. What is inside? She knows that a body was placed in the grave before her. Has a perfect soul escaped from that crack, she ponders, leaving in its wake perfect bones? But clean bones do not explain the flies' nagging presence. Flies are dirt-eaters, Aunt has told her often. They eat rotten things, they revel in de-compo-sition and where they settle to feed, they lay eggs—eggs that transform themselves into worms. Charlotte supposed that if the eggs of chickens were a gift of Light, the eggs of flies must be the gift of Darkness.

She thinks of all the flies she has ever seen collecting upon the indecipherable lumps of neglected chicken offal that Edma wrenches from the gaping corpses of chickens and throws into the kitchen yard—for the chickens. If chickens eat one another just as evil persons do (Edma had pointed out such people in an illustrated newspaper article she had saved—sullen creatures with extravagantly knobby knees protruding grotesquely from beneath scanty grass skirts and despised by God for having devoured all their neighbors) how can their eggs possibly be clean? That morning, Charlotte comes to the irrevocable conclusion that eggs are not fit for human consumption.

"Aunt!" she suddenly cries, forgetting that she must never interrupt Edma in prayer. "Aunt! Where does the *meat* go?"

Her question is answered by a nasty pinch on the cheek that leaves a mark, red and white, for many throbbing minutes. Charlotte wonders if cannibals eat family members and through silent tears gazes intently upon her mother's grave. For the first time she sees that the wreath of glass beads moored there is shaped like an open mouth—a vertical mouth—quite large enough for Charlotte to pass through. Is the mouth a door? Did her mother's soul pass through that door on its way to Heaven? After reflection, she decides that the mouth, having eaten and digested her mother's meat, having sucked her bones clean, allowed her soul to escape as a sigh from its lips, leaving a perfect skeleton behind. She sees that every grave has a wreath and this confirms her discovery. (No wreath is visible on the façade of the mausoleum and this very neatly explains the presence of those spectacularly numerous flies.)

Many years later, Charlotte will enter the mausoleum alone. She will find a wreath inside, but broken, its twisted wire frame having rusted and crumbled, the glass pearls, silver, blue and white, strewn across the tilted floor.

It is time to go home. Charlotte walks towards the gate sandwiched between her aunt and uncle. She sees a small bird perched naughtily on a cross; a moon-shaped stone broken in two like a wafer; smells the lush scent of chrysanthemums—those gallic flowers of death—and boxwood. And then she perceives a faint but persistent odor that, sickly sweet, frightens her and has to do with the unusually warm day, *the heat, the meat, it dies, it flies* . . . and they are passing the poorer graves, all marked off by squares of pink gravel, scalloped on the edges like fancy birthday cakes.

> *The Four Hours of the Day,*
> *Morning, Noon, Evening and Night,*
> *The Square proclaims God's might.*

Unexpectedly, Edma stoops and carefully pulls up a small grey-green plant by the roots—a perennial she intends to add to the kitchen yard's flower borders. Charlotte, choking on suppressed curiosity, takes advantage of the unexpected gesture and asks:

"Aunt, what does e.t.e.r.n.a.l. mean?"

"E-E-E-ternal!" Emile stutters.

"Eternal," says Edma, pleased to answer a question she considers worthwhile, "is Forever. Like God."

"F-F-F-" Emile adds.

"Is He *Death,* Aunt?"

"He is Death and He is Life. He takes and He gives. For example, when you were born, your mother died."

"Why did He make her *die?*"

"She sinned against Him!"

"L-L-L-Lust!" explains Emile.

Charlotte did not know what lust was, but she imagined it was not unlike cannibalism. She wished with all her heart that God would die. She would steal his wreath so that His soul and His bones and His meat would rot together. Forever. So that flies would feed upon His corpse. Forever. And that night Charlotte dreamed her own triangle.

It was immense, rising from the sands of a vast desert. When she approached, she discovered that it was actually a pyramid and so large that once she had walked around it she was terribly tired, hot and thirsty. She wondered if it had a door, so that she could enter and lie down in the shade. But looking closely, she saw that it was made of pieces of red meat, sewn together with thick black thread, and that the whole thing stank of rotten chicken offal. Suddenly the thread bloomed with blue flies, and the sound of their buzzing was deafening.

"Aunt! Aunt!" she cried, frightened. "What is it?" But a voice that was not her aunt's voice replied:

It is the House of God.

CHAPTER
10

Charlotte vomited often, although she ate seldom, and, when she did, sparsely. Her crippled heart would all at once spring up and pound quite as vigorously as the church bell during the weekly celebrations of marriage and death—so vigorously, in fact, it could be seen leaping beneath her impeccably ironed white linen blouses. Her temples would throb and she would experience a hot flush, a tingling in her cheeks, as if her face had been slapped. Then a chill, rising from the base of her spine in irresistible waves to the nape of her neck, would flow fan-wise out to each ear. It was like being inhabited by a luminous tree. But the best was the way it felt when it was all over, and she left empty and clean: clean as a whistle.

As she ate very little, Charlotte's vomit was invariably clear, almost like water. This meant unqualified sympathy from her Aunt Edma. She would be washed and plied with sweet apple cider and forbidden dishes of stewed fruit. These she would refuse with a limp shake of the head; tremulously she would ask for tepid water. New exclamations of concern would rain down upon her as manna:

"Water! Imagine! The angel lives on water and air! The little nun!" and so on. For as other children thrive on gravy and mashed potatoes, the delicate Charlotte thrived on these exemplary moments. Special treats did not tempt her; it was her aunt's fear for her life she slavered for.

She would vomit, therefore, her own troubled, inoffensive cocktail; and after much ceremony and a sip of lukewarm water, would be put to bed. There, carefully tucked between two crisp sheets and matching coverlet, she would lie and listen to the ticking of the little green clock poised on the dresser at the far corner of the room, and watch its dear little arms turn ever so slowly.

In the center of Charlotte's clock stood a smiling dwarf; one of his arms was slender and long, the other thick and truncated. Not surprisingly, this maimed arm moved far more slowly than the other.

Charlotte's pale head, with its large, brooding eyes, is framed by a plump lace-edged pillow. She smiles to herself, knowing that in time a warm rice gruel, served in a porcelain porringer, will be brought to her; that a second equally satisfactory pillow will be fetched from the dresser to prop up her head, and that with much cooing, the gruel will be coaxed between her transparent lips. Eyes glued to the ceiling, Charlotte will accept this meager dish, knowing that it is all she really needs to sustain herself.

Charlotte rolls her head to the side and examines her pillow. Experienced, she knows that within seconds a miraculous transformation will occur and it does; the pillow, rising gently away from her cheek, takes on the aspect of finely grained snow that swells towards a distant horizon of frosted woods and towers. Leisurely she explores these mysteries with mind and eye, projecting herself as a minikin cavalier who—her trusty dwarf plodding at her side—confronts the lace border with equanimity.

Safe in bed she dares wander thus; the plump coverlet, the bedside table with its ready water glass, the certainty that warm food will appear presently, all protect her; as does the time: five o'clock—that most tranquil of hours.

A rosy light filters through the graceful curtains, and the linoleum, with its visions of speckled fowl amid florid branches, is faded and glossy.

Yes, thinks Charlotte, I am safe.

Her belly is empty. The gruel has not yet come and she, having vomited, is as clean as a whistle. And that means Death is far away. But is it? Is Death ever far away? Perhaps, like God, Death is Everywhere. Concealed in the towers of an enchanted horizon, a silent bird of prey watching from the fabulous branches of rare trees. Or simply ticking away in a little green clock. And for the first time, Charlotte looks at her one and only playmate with suspicion. The dwarf's foolish face, the face she loves, troubles her. His smile, no longer playful and all at once ironic, is more of a smirk than a smile. The droll hat pointing to Heaven is too pointed, almost sharp, as if hewn of metal. And the arms! Those beloved arms! The one so fat and squat is very much like the soldier's arm she had seen at the train station (its odd little sleeve tucked and pinned so neatly!); and the other, long and thin, is as thin as the arm of the organ-grinder who passes beneath her window on Saturday afternoons with a ratty, red-skirted lady ape, begging for apples and rags. Hadn't Edma called that man a Crafty Devil? And the ape a Thing of Hell?

Charlotte pulls herself up from her pillow and stares. Automatically, she puts her hand to her heart and wonders if she is going to be sick. But this thought is fleeting, for now all her attention is riveted to the clock. Yes! The swift arm, thin as a blade and as sharp, is very like the organ-grinder's arm, and the other—why, it has been lopped right off! Have the two arms fought each other? If so, the faster has clearly won. Where will it strike next? How ugly the little dwarf is! How rudely he grins! And Charlotte's heart pounds beneath her nightdress so loudly that the ticking of the clock is now imperceptible.

"I will show him!" Charlotte cries, frightened by the sound of her own high and quaking voice. And again, louder: "I *will* show him!" She runs to the dresser to grab the clock and hurl it against the wall where it splinters into a hundred bits and pieces.

"There!" she sobs in terror. "There! You see! I was faster!" And in triumph, she smashes the bits with her fist.

At once she pulls back, for she has badly cut herself. Fascinated, she stares as the blood drips from her hand in large, dark drops. She sucks hard, spitting out a shard that has caught to the flesh, and looks on stunned as the cleanly sucked wounds well up with new blood. She sucks again and again, discovering that her blood is warm and sweet; Charlotte thinks that she has never tasted anything sweeter.

"I am wounded!" she whispers, dizzy with excitement. "This is my own blood!" And the sight of it affords her an insight into the terrible nature of her own intimate being: Charlotte has never been as clean as a whistle. Only dead things are that clean—old bones and empty bottles.

Holding her hand to her mouth she pokes through the pieces that lay scattered upon the floor. The metal parts she gathers together into a pile and hides under the mattress. The glass remains; fearing discovery but, above all, craving a thing that has always crouched silently within her, its face hidden, now visible, she, with the help of the near-full water pitcher and her own drinking glass, swallows it all. And the feeling of glass going down her unwilling throat affords her a strange and terrible satisfaction. She thinks of the Princess who weeps diamonds; she, Charlotte, swallows glass. She knows her deed is the greater; more perilous by far, it is above all unprecedented. As Edma enters, the little porcelain porringer glowing like the Grail between her hands, Charlotte vomits blood, ropes of it, exultant.

CHAPTER

11

Once the Exorcist had witnessed the decapitation of a female assassin. Kissed on the lips by its executioner, the severed head had blushed with indignation.

Within the intimate grotto beneath Charlotte's bed, his task the scrupulous inquiry into the nature of dust, the Exorcist clutches his pulsing prick and ruminates. He has read that certain parts of the body are corrupted more quickly than others: the cranium's grey jelly survives long after the rest of the body has putrefied, and the scattered limbs of martyrs are celebrated for their capacity to withstand the ravages of beasts and time. The Exorcist himself had seen displayed, in the basilica of Padua, Saint Anthony's tongue—rosy red and rigid—long after that voluble holy man had turned to dust. He savors the recollection of its flagrant nudity; a crystal dome magnified the tongue's knobbly surface. Dry (and he did not doubt, hot), the tongue, analogous to asparagus, was exemplarily *masculine* and therefore diametrically opposed to the base lettuce, unstable, wet, *female*—so rightly despised by the Pythagoreans.

Considering Saint Anthony's promiscuous tongue and the improbity of feminine foliages, he lifts the catch and passes through the Garden Gate of Pleasure, moving his fist from fruit to root, from fruit to root; the throbbing memory of that triumphal tongue fills his heart, his hand. . . .

Am I deceived? he wonders feebly, spilling semen all over the linoleum. Overindulgence (including the excessive consumption of lettuce) leads to Impotence. His member, still in his hand, has wilted.

"O Abraxas!" he pleads. "Am I unworthy?" The study of Saint Anthony has taught him that speech is the only form of seduction free from corruption.

"Your Disgrace! O Wheel of Fire! Accept the tribute of an ailing man!" He knows that to catch an eagle he must play at being prey; to catch a vulture he must play at being dead. Was his Master Eagle or Vulture? Was he both?

"All is peril," he mutters, semen drying on his trembling fingers.

". . . And just what is it you see? In the dust beneath her bed?" At the end of the afternoon, it is customary for Edma to serve the Exorcist a copious snack which comprises his only meal. (Indeed, since Charlotte's illness, he has not had to furnish the distinguished professors of Natural History of Tours with toads to buy his bread, nor tramp into the back country in foul weather to unknot the hexed penises of unfortunate husbands.) Dropping a fistful of pale brown sugar cubes into his tea, the Exorcist answers, his mouth nearly incapacitated by angel food cake.

"Albert the Great owned a Talking Head of bronze which—under the threat of Fire—answered all his questions. The head's been lost, but I have Dust, Humble Dust to answer mine. It has mystic properties and indicates to me the names of those infernal larvae who tug at the strings of Charlotte's destiny. I've seeded the floorboards this afternoon with the clay of a smashed golem and with crushed *Hippophlomos*. . . ."

"Hippophlomos?"

"Better known as the Mandragore. The *thinking* vegetable, gifted with will and damned with passion! Yes! I seed the dust with Hippophlomos, ground together with golem stuff and the tears of angels. . . . Her case," he confided, "is unusual."

"Unusual?"

"Martyrs are by custom inspired by the agony of the Christ. But the Green Dwarf of whom she speaks when delirious is clearly an envoy of Satan. Obviously, despite her somber origins, her luminosity is offensive to Beelzebub!"

"The Green Dwarf, oddly enough," Edma admitted, "was a little figure she was once very fond of—painted on a small clock."

"Aha!" He was excited. "And where is this clock?"

"I believe," Edma whispered, "that Charlotte may have eaten it."

"Eaten her clock!" He clapped his hands together. "And so the glass she spat. . . ."

"The clock's face."

"Think of that!" he marveled. "The clock's face!"

"I found the rest—the springs and such—beneath her mattress this morning!"

"I'll need them!" he said.

"The child is mad," said Edma, "and a burden. Better that it had died along with the mother."

For many long hours, Charlotte tarries in the petrified gardens of drugged sleep. The Exorcist has painted the soles of her feet with the orange dung of Persian parakeets; she has been force-fed an execrable soup of sour milk and black poppy seeds, peppered with iron filings. A magnetized cross has been placed over her heart.

"For," as she has overheard the Exorcist explain to Edma, "Charlotte has lost her polarity and must be grounded."

Charlotte holds the cross in abject terror. She believes it to be an extension of the organ-grinder's body, a Satanic limb. What, she weeps, knowing in her marrow the answer, does the organ-grinder *grind?* She confuses him (and by extension the Green Dwarf) with her cure, but: The antidote to many an ill is poison. (Edma.)

In fact, it was Emile who had saved Charlotte's life with a dish of stewed leek; the fibers had knotted themselves about the splinters of glass.

In her battle with the Green Dwarf, Charlotte has fractured her voice. She can no longer speak above a whisper, she cannot say Christ nor Glory, but with Edma at her bedside she prays to Jesus; she can no more say: Holy.

> *O Father, Son and Spirit*
> *Spirit of the True Cross of Heaven*
> *Spirit of the True Cross of the Sky*
> *Protect me from Death:*
> *Wasps in my head,*
> *Stones in my bed.*
> *Amen.*

If the Green Dwarf has taken Charlotte's voice, he has in exchange given her the gift of Second Sight. How many times throughout the long months of her convalescence has she seen the walls buckle and tear as the Mother of God swims into her room as quietly as an undulating jellyfish to show her the globe of the world in miniature, its lapis lazuli oceans and chalcedony continents spinning in the billowing folds of her mantle as upon clouds? And Charlotte has seen Edma's name knotted and unknotted upon the lizarded ceiling, a magic formula linking itself there fleetingly but repeatedly and with unforgettable clarity:

M
M A
M A D
M A D E
M A D E D
M A D E D M
M A D E D M A

This afternoon, Charlotte wakes to see a two-dimensional Christ—his arms outstretched before him—floating beneath the ceiling, his white body dissolving like sugar in water, his lonely eyes suspended in the air like pearls. Then turning her head she sees a lady ape exploring the cracked linoleum with a pin. Only after several fearful minutes of scrutiny does she recognize the Exorcist. He holds a little set of copper scales and appears to be weighing small particles of dust.

My intended! he breathes when raising his eyes he sees that she is awake and watching him. She who dares eat the face of Time!

"What . . . eu! Ah! Are you doing?" Charlotte manages to whisper.

"My little *crotte!*" he cries, grabbing her feet from under the blanket and pressing them to his heart. "You see before you a lover of the contemplative life! Immobile and Silent as you sleep I pass the hours reading our future in your bedchamber's dirt!"

CHAPTER
12

Even before meeting Charlotte, the Mother Superior was convinced that this child, dramatically marked from birth—who had *eaten glass*—was a rare clay body destined for Purification in the fiery kiln of Beatitude. She was interested in Martyrdom professionally, and stunning cases, all book-learned, came to mind. She sincerely believed that it was only the punished bodies that received visits from God.

The "Good Mother," as the novices called her, supervised St.-Gemmes, a vast, moldering edifice that had been constructed in the fifteenth century upon a depression of blasted land halfway between Louerre and La Folie, where nothing had ever been seen to grow, and where, as local custom would have it, God Himself had long ago, in mighty, choleric excess, sent hurtling the burning gallstone of His disillusion.

All is Torment, the Good Mother was often heard to groan, Travail, Exhaustion, Doubt and Need. The dangling, the lonely and the shy were her vocation, and the strange; in her narcissistic frenzies she sucked them quite dry. Many were the novices who floundered upon the banks of her esteem. The rules of her realm were rigorous; above the gate it was written:

> *When He does violence to our spirit*
> *It is only because He must bend us to His modulations.*

In the past God had sent her many startling gifts: a double-yolked egg on her breakfast tray, a smooth pebble in her plate of hash, the grimacing corpse of a mummified cat uncovered in the masonry, the pornographic engraving fallen to the library floor from a nonexistent volume, the artifacts left behind in the cupboard by the previous Mother Superior: a peaked hat, an iron girdle, a wand; all those weird scraps spilled from the edge of Other Reality and into her life—the girl with the forked tongue who had died whistling hymns, the one with the cleft palate who never slept and who expired, an old, wrinkled crone, at the age of twelve, the Siamese twins Adeline and Elisée, joined together at the tiny, fallible heart they shared; the hissing balls of fire that danced above her bed at night, the macabre nightmares—whose stunning tableaux of torture and rape (genital flagellation with the Crown of Thorns one of the most troubling) reminded her that the Path to Righteousness is cluttered with Temptation. Penitent, she had rubbed her clitoris with nettles and crept about naked on all fours in the cold of her unkept rooms until ill, but her illness only led her further astray, or so she believed, for then her thoughts became disconnected, ragged flags flapping in the wind, and the nettle's sting excited her. Later, when she thought of how she had thrashed the nettles against her vulva and thighs and even (Heaven Forbid!) jammed the whole, stinging, juicy bunch *into* herself, she knelt before the Beloved Bridegroom and with great pain of heart pleaded for Charity. She believed that the price of Redemption was Disgrace.

That afternoon, the Mother Superior pulled on her galoshes and set out for La Folie—a full hour's walk from St.-Gemmes. All the way she prayed and when she was not praying she planned just what she would say and just how she would say it, with what gestures of the hands, general attitudes, expressions of the eyes and lips—to be all at once seductive, convincing, consistent and above all, consistently astounding.

CHAPTER
13

It was Easter and the Mother Superior brought Charlotte a hollow sugar egg with a cellophane window. Charlotte was asleep when she arrived and the egg was left on her bedside table.

Charlotte awoke towards early evening. Illuminated by the setting sun, the dust in the air glittered down upon her. Her squalid dresser was stippled with gold, and the sunlight, bouncing from the window glass, oozed in sticky oblong drops from the faded, papered walls. For the first time in many months she awoke at peace. As she lay moored in enchantment, she wondered if her soul, like her dresser, had been transformed by light. Then Charlotte saw the egg.

When she reached out for it and felt its hard, granular husk, she was so frightened she nearly dropped it to the floor. Was this a new vision? Gingerly she brought the egg close to her face; perceiving its little window, she shut one eye and peeked inside. There she saw, in a nest of straw, a mother hen and her chicks suspended in a turquoise sky beneath a silver star. On a paper banner above this scene it was written: What came first? The chicken or the egg?

To Charlotte the answer was at once evident. Chicken and egg are simultaneous phenomena. The one embraces the promise of the other. But the question thrilled her because it implied that beyond the trite reality of Edma's kitchen yard lay another reality. Like her visions, the egg's window afforded a new image of the world. And all at once *Charlotte knew God.* Simply, He was that window. Holding the egg to her cheek, Charlotte smiled; and like the infant phoenix, a worm engendered by ashes, she rose and shook Death from her wings.

When she appeared in the kitchen, unsteady on skinny legs, Emile was alone. His secret vice was to dip a cube of sugar into a spoonful of cognac and eat it. He was doing this now.

"Emile," Charlotte whispered, "may I have an eu-eu *ekk?*"

As Charlotte spooned the perfect softness of a four-minute egg into her mouth, well seasoned with salt and fresh butter, Edma accompanied the Mother Superior to the edge of La Folie and the road that led to St.-Gemmes. Before returning home, she stopped at the Exorcist's house, which stood slanting just beside the church.

The house, like its inhabitant, was spindly and it was also very dark. Mice had eaten all the candles and the Exorcist had himself imbibed the little kerosene remaining in the lamps. When Edma found him standing in the obscurity of his squalid kitchen, he was attempting to photograph his own rear end in the uncertain light of a high, miserly window. She at once averted her head.

"*Everything* must be on record . . ." he explained. Edma stood impatiently waiting for him to finish, her eyes tactfully glued to the moldy wall.

". . . else the Universe fall apart. I've counted over four hundred species of mold on that wall alone," he continued, following her gaze, "and this morning—stuck to the soles of my own shoes—sixteen sorts of dog hair! The sheddings of sixteen dogs? Or of one multicolored cur? Who is to say? The Devil alone knows. I am but a scribe . . . I do the best

I can." And turning his posterior to the camera's eye, he squeezed the rubber pear.

"I've just had a visit from the Mother Superior!" Edma cut in with exasperation. "She is *very* interested in Charlotte and has asked that I send her to St.-Gemmes in the fall."

"I *knew* it!" he said, not to be outdone.

"I told her that I'd think about it," Edma said, "wanting to talk it over with you first."

"A brilliant move," he decided, methodically probing his nose with his little finger. "I've wanted to penetrate those vestal wastes for years. I say send her!"

"I agree," Edma said at once. "Such a peculiar, provoking child! God knows what she'll do next! This morning she asked for a silver thimble—to keep her tears in! But . . . if we send her away, who can be trusted to collect her nail parings? And the dust beneath her bed? Remove the Stain?"

"The Stain is a signature, I have told you. It is meant to stay! To be read! I have read the future in that ink!" he confided, and dramatically covering his mouth with both hands before continuing he added: "But it is too soon for me to say just what it is I have read. . . . Yes! The Stain is writing its own history. We will send her to St.-Gemmes. And I will follow."

"But . . . a convent! And you . . . a man!"

"You forget, I have Powers!" he whispered provocatively. "And I can turn myself into just about anything! A shoe! A mouse! A *mold.* . . ."

Edma looked anxiously at the spotted stones. "I'll inform Charlotte at once!" she said to the floor, and grabbing up her skirts she fled from the house.

Seduced by the Mother Superior's gift and its message of transcendence, Charlotte did not question her destiny. The name St.-Gemmes engendered vistas of sanctity encrusted with jewels. There Mystery nourished Body *and* Soul—had not the mere sight of the sugar egg revived her? Throughout the lengthening afternoons she lay in bed, her expanding daydream an intimation of the expanding universe. And all the Exorcist's gnostic rantings of resting places—the World perceived as Inn, an oasis stuck like a plum in the uncertain pudding of transmigration—all came to focus on St.-Gemmes. In those idle hours, Charlotte constructed a world where girls washed clean in the Seas of Compassion, having mastered the primary alphabets, the languages of flower, fish and beast, the stunning vocabularies of minerals, conversed with the stars. Freed from the bonds of Body, they entered the constellation of Mind to straddle with ease that coveted celestial broomstick named Grace.

Throughout this time, the nightmare of the Green Dwarf was usurped by a churchy vision of fairyland—or rather a fairyland vision of the Church. The Mother Superior, who had made it her duty to visit Charlotte each week, barely understood her precocious babble, obstructed as it was by a speech impediment. But what she did grasp caused her to marvel and to rejoice: Charlotte spoke poetry, she spoke in metaphor, and the Holy Mother responded in like manner, feeding her pupil's imagination with her own garbled moonshine of Sainthood, Heavenly Splendor and Infinite Love. She had unearthed a ruby, inexpertly cut, fumbled and scratched, but of unquestionable quality. She was certain that the severity of St.-Gemmes would polish those rough surfaces. The spirit within would be made to shine forth, illuminating God's Glory, the Glory of St.-Gemmes, and above all, the Glory of the Mother Superior. Hallelujah! she sang within herself after these visits. What a prize! What a prize!

"Your ordeal, the limpidity of your soul, the devastating humility of your act of violence upon your mortal husk,

Charlotte, brings to mind examples among your contemporaries. Girls who, like yourself, trod His Thorny Paths.

"I've heard tell of one Mademoiselle Cloche, a chronic sufferer of lockjaw; her only sustenance, the weekly Eucharist. For fourteen years, she's eaten nothing else! And sweet, melancholic Madeline, who each Friday since 1872 has bled at the brow from wounds inflicted by an invisible crown of thorns."

"Euh . . . she must suffer terribly!" said Charlotte.

"Inexpressibly! And there is Palma, Pious Palma, who to save her native city from volcanic eruption burns! When Palma succumbs to seizure her bed linens ignite!

"The thought of these True Spirits, Charlotte, so touching in Torment, should excite emulation. In the celestial Jerusalem their souls will shine as suns! Let us pray that Divine Justice . . ." she lowered her voice, ". . . will judge us worthy to shine with them. If not, we will be excluded. Excluded forever." She kissed Charlotte's damp cheek and closing the door softly behind her went down the stairs to Edma's kitchen.

Charlotte pulled her covers tightly around herself and clenched her teeth. *No!* she promised herself; I will not be excluded!

"I think you should know," said Edma to the Mother Superior over a cup of freshly filtered coffee, "the family history. For you see, as the Exorcist has explained to me, the Stain is indeed a signature—an imprint of the mother's sin—a cosmic negative so to speak. (The Exorcist is, among other things, a consummate photographer—oh! a *very* gifted man!) Now my niece—may she be damned! (For Hell must serve a purpose, Ma Soeur, must it not?) She was," Edma confided in a hoarse whisper, "totally depraved! No better than a whore! And the daughter of a whore! And a raving madwoman to boot—finished her life in a cage! Oh I'd warned my brother. You see, I knew from the start. I could *smell* the sin on her! And the way she laughed—showed all her teeth, you could see clear down her throat! Wayward baggage! I tell you, she'd knock around town with her hair in braids like a Touareg and wag her tail like a mare! I told him, I said, Marry that demoness and be damned! But you know men, ruled by lust! And then—everybody knows—one morning she showed up at Mass stark naked!" Edma stopped, frowning, not because she had said too much but because the subject of her sister-in-law, of whom she was consumed with envy even now, so enraged her. "Both creatures—my sister-in-law and my niece—were depraved! Hussies! Trollops! Well, they are all dead now," she added with some satisfaction.

The Mother Superior tilted her head to one side and smiled with great warmth, taking Edma's hand into her own.

"Madame," she said, "I would be very grateful if you would be so kind as to introduce me to the Exorcist. This must remain a secret—his unorthodoxy has made him something of a black sheep in our little community."

Edma felt a twinge of jealousy. Until now she had shared the Exorcist with no one. And yet, Charlotte's destiny was at stake and the Exorcist's influence upon the Mother Superior (and therefore on St.-Gemmes) could only be salutary.

"I shall arrange it," said Edma.

When Charlotte was well enough, Edma walked her to the church to pray for full recovery. Holding Charlotte by the arm, she guided her quickly past the great white columns of stone upon which the naked bodies of sinners could clearly be seen roasting in the fires of Hell; and the full-breasted figures of sirens, of wolves devouring a criosphynx, of diabolic fornications—figures, Edma feared, that could only give Charlotte more odd ideas. How irritating it was! Again and again she had asked the priest to knock them off with a hammer, or to plaster them over, or at least to have them draped with cloth.

Edma led Charlotte into a chilly chapel called the Chapel of Miracles; its walls were cluttered with marble plaques offered in thanks to the virgin and its atmosphere dim with candlefire. She sat Charlotte down in one of the many old chairs and wrapped her up like a chrysalis in a prickly wool blanket. Then, having lifted her skirts to her face, Edma fell to her knees and made her way from the chapel down into the transept's north arm, down the north aisle and across the nave into the south aisle, the transept's south arm, the ambulatory and the apse, and on into the axial chapels—turning around and about, around and about, in a harrowing ritual that lasted well over two hours and left her panting for breath and her knees badly bruised.

Meanwhile Charlotte looked into Mary's blind face hoping to be recognized, at the swollen brass heart that hung from her neck by a clock spring (a detail of particular significance to Charlotte); at her naked feet, at the cross rooted between her legs, at the gilded mantle that rose in a breath of frozen wind, floating about her shoulders, and at the light that spilled into the chapel from three round stained-glass windows.

By Mary's side stood a small plaster statue of Saint Anthony. Pray to him, Edma had insisted; he's the one who can give you back your voice. But Saint Anthony had an ugly blue beard and crossed eyes besides, and Charlotte prayed to Mary, to the little brass heart that shone between her breasts like a tiny planet, and even to the light that stirred and hummed upon the worn, faded carpet giving blossoms to its stained branches and threadbare roots.

"Mother Mary," she mumbled, making up the words as she went along,

"Mother Mary, 'oly Light
Take me in your lovely boat
Away from the night . . .
And . . . and . . . uh
Give me back my . . . uh!
Broken throat.
Amen."

CHAPTER
14

It was a busy week. Edma prepared for the meeting of the Mother Superior and the Exorcist in a state of perpetual agitation verging on hysteria. She washed everything— walls, ceilings, floors, the insides of closets. She soaked, starched and ironed all the curtains, beat with ferocity carpets and cushions; every wood surface was waxed (as was the ubiquitous linoleum); every object of metal, from chair tacks to brass doorknobs, rubbed to an unearthly shine, and the fat foliage of houseplants shone beneath a fresh veil of mayonnaise. Only once everything was under perfect control did she prepare the menu, and the list of things she would need to buy from the greengroceress.

The Mother Superior and the Exorcist had been invited for Sunday dinner—as ritual dictated, a protracted, noontime affair, broached by veal-bone broth, followed by vegetable salads and cold sliced meats, in turn trailed by a stew; a roast succeeded by dressed lettuce, cheeses attending, cake concluding (and fruit, sweets and coffee). Edma, who fretted for weeks over the smallest of unnecessary expenditures, who spent white nights in penance over the leanest of luxuries, had decided, this one time, to hang the expense. Even the best wines from Emile's cellar would be roused from their mossy slumbers.

Edma and Emile discussed the menu for several days; rather Edma talked and Emile nodded, nodded and salivated, salivated and nodded, not believing his good fortune. A feast! He had not feasted since the wedding. Emile's belly roared. For lunch Edma had prepared carrot soup.

"E-E-E-Ed-eu?" he stuttered.

"Yes, Emile?" she said, not looking up from her list. "Out with it!"

"Coo-coo-could . . . p-p-per-perhapsss . . . a cass . . . a cass-oo-oo-oo?"

"A cassoulet! What nonsense! You need fat goose for that, *confit,* where do you expect me to find *confit?* Cassoulet! God give me patience! *Imbecile!*"

Wearily Emile left the kitchen to putter in the garden. After a time he went to the toolshed—the only place Edma never entered (ever since a startled shrew had scrambled up her leg)—and from a forbidding clutter he pulled out the box of knives. He placed it on his worktable beneath a small dirty window and for a few minutes, his eyes closed, simply caressed its flanks. Beneath Emile's work-worn palms the leather felt as soft as the skin of a lovely young woman.

"M-my b-beauty!" he breathed.

He then opened the box and one by one removed the knives and saluted them in turn. For each knife had a name: Arsène, Gildas, Fritz, Mademoiselle de Maintenant, Gilles de Rais. . . .

CHAPTER
15

As Charlotte was now strong enough for short walks, Edma took her along to the grocery to fetch the provisions for Sunday dinner. On their way they were passed by the Téton twins who were chattering happily together, their arms enlaced about each other's waists. Charlotte had never seen the twins, but Edma had told her frightening things about them, convinced that they were dangerous aberrations. They were known to turn salt pork and fresh milk sour. Yet they expressed such delight in one another, such passion as they talked, clinging together, that Charlotte decided, not without envy, that the twins had God.

"Ka–Ka Cröac!" one twin cried into the ear of the other.

"Kristmax! Kristmax!" replied his brother, pointing to the sky. And Charlotte thought that it would be a blessing to share a private language that no one else could understand.

"Emile," she whispered to her aunt, "talks to his cabbages!"

Edma slapped her hard, gloved hand across Charlotte's face (to hide the Stain or her eyes, it was not clear to Charlotte which).

"Monsters!" Edma hissed, crossing herself.

One entered the grocery directly from the cobblestone street; there was no sidewalk, but a thick slab of pink granite that served as a step. The front door was pierced with little panes of smoked glass; to each side windows of the same glass had been set, through which one caught tempting glimpses of the marvels for sale within: glass jars of chocolates in the shapes of shoes, dried plums and raisins, almonds, fresh coffee, red, white and yellow string, jet beads and buttons, embroidery canvases printed with scenes of pastoral felicity, flower baskets and cathedrals, songbirds, the Angelus and the Mona Lisa; a vermilion pencil box, a silver pyramid of canned sardines stamped with emerald-green views of exotic seaports.

Edma pushed the door open, and to the sound of a jingling bell Charlotte's nostrils were assailed by cow and goat cheese, pork and beef sausage, honeycomb, lavender, mildew, starch and cat piss. (The greengroceress owned a large and beautiful long-haired puss—a fearless ratter and affectionate, but sloppy in her personal habits.)

As Charlotte stood rocking upon wave after wave of pure olfactory ecstasy, her eyes wandered across the counter, into corners, along shelves. The shop was painted apple-green and the shelves, all lined with ivory paper, were fronted with glass. Each thing thus framed was favored with mystery, from the brown cubes of laundry soap (a grinning cat's head printed on one side), to the flat pink envelopes of cornstarch. She promised herself that she would examine each item carefully before moving on to the next, but fresh delights winked and twinkled from all sides at once.

"Well! Well!" the greengroceress chuckled as she entered the shop from behind the counter, bringing with her new smells from her spicy kitchen. "Look who's out and about! Our little lame sparrow, and as thin as a twig! Hungry, Charlotte? Hungry for some warm applecake?" Charlotte nodded. "Well then!" she cried, "come sit in the kitchen where it's sunny and have a slice!" And drying her red hands in the deep folds of her immaculate apron, she grabbed Charlotte's wrist and led her into the fragrant kitchen before Edma could complain or comply. Charlotte saw the oilcloth gleaming liquidly in the sun, the cake still pleasantly steaming, a windowsill garden of basil and chives and the cat coiled like a caterpillar beside the stove. Glued fast with pleasure, she stood smiling as the greengroceress, with much promising clatter, fetched a fork and a plate from a cupboard the size of a small house.

"Charlotte cannot eat rich food!" Edma stood trembling in the doorway. Charlotte stared at the kitchen wallpaper's scattered lemon-yellow scenes of fishermen and oyster feasts, and bit her lip.

"But a little fresh cake surely won't hurt her? The best butter and . . ."

"Charlotte is an invalid."

"Well. She can drink some milk." The greengroceress was herself a woman of energy and resented being bullied. Once Edma had turned her back, she slipped Charlotte an orange. She had never eaten oranges—they were imported and very expensive—and not knowing how to approach it, left it untouched. Alone with the cat, Charlotte sipped her milk cautiously and admired a bone china caravan—sleep-walkers proceeding with the slowness of stones across the kitchen mantle.

CHAPTER
16

The metal tub had been hauled from the yard and brought into the kitchen where Edma had scrubbed Charlotte raw with a pig-bristle brush. When she had finished Charlotte's skin was bleeding, her nails pared to the stinging quick, and her hair—washed and rinsed with vinegar—had been pulled into tight paper shells, a curling iron applied, her neck and ears singed, her temper tried and above all her pride rankled: Edma had insisted upon an enema of holy water. But now it was over and Charlotte sat stiff and silent in a fantastically overstarched dress. When Edma stepped back to look her over with a critical eye, lingering with beetled brows upon the Stain, Charlotte knew that the soap, brush and curling iron had not absolved her from her inheritance.

Edma rummaged in a drawer and then approached Charlotte aggressively with a box of pale yellow powder.

"I must do something to it—it gets bigger every day! Sit *still!*" Edma began to scrub away at the Stain with the powderpuff, maneuvering it like sandpaper.

"No!" Charlotte cried. "*No!*" And with her eyes squeezed shut against the powder she pushed Edma away, sending the box spilling to the floor. With all the strength of her tiny frame of iron and wire Edma slapped Charlotte's face.

"I 'ate oo!" Charlotte screamed as best she could with her mangled throat. "I ate oo!" And as Edma dragged her kicking up the stairs to lock her away in her room she ranted: "I ate oo! I ate oo!"

The door slammed shut, Charlotte fell to the linoleum in a heap. For a long time she lay there, sobbing; the Stain— like a scrap of dark velvet pressed beneath a very hot iron— burned the palm of her hand.

Later she heard the key turn in the lock. To her relief, it was Emile's hand that touched her shoulder. He bent down and took her in his arms, rocking her.

"Li-li-little!" he soothed. "Loo-loo-look!" Charlotte shook her head. "Loo-look!" Emile insisted. She opened her eyes. In the center of Emile's worn palm glowed a ripe strawberry. The first of spring; she knew he had been caring for it like a baby. She threw her arms around his scruffy neck and clung to him as he patted and rubbed her back tenderly, smearing her dress with fruit.

CHAPTER

17

The veal-bone broth was set before each guest and a zig-gurat of freshly sliced bread, tender and crackling, dominated the table's center with Babylonian prodigality (the Exorcist).

"Master," the Exorcist intoned, "we know these delights are but enticements, seductions of an all too easily corrupted flesh. But if the fruit of nature is of infernal origin, the culinary arts are themselves blessèd. Freed from the grip of Appetite, Spirit flies, the tongue transcends itself. Did not Saint Anthony himself savor with that exalted particular the Devil's own provender transmuted to sanctity in the athanors of monasticity?"

"Oh!" breathed the Mother Superior. "How well you expressed that!"

"*Ingenio formae damna rependo meae,*" he replied: "My spiritual gifts are recompense for my lack of beauty." And breaking bread into his dish and eagerly watching as it floated upon the surface of the broth, added: "And so it swells."

"Yes?" wondered the Mother Superior.

"The bread! So it swells in broth! As, Madame, my heart swells in the mere contemplation of this beautiful soup. Indeed as does my soul, wallowing (so to speak) in such felicitous odoriferosity!" And, breathing in deeply:

"All is Breath. Where would mankind be without his

lungs? And where would he be," he added, delighting in his rhyme and bringing his spoon to his lips, "without his tongue?" And he set to with gusto. The Mother Superior, herself warmed by the soup, the talk, the promise of roast duckling that lay heavily upon the air, bravely offered her own witticism:

"*Ignitum eloquium tuum vehementer;* your verb is consuming fire!"

But this he in no way acknowledged, taken up as he was in the enjoyment of his soup.

"Appetite!" he cried, sponging up the little broth remaining with a fresh slice of bread. "All is Appetite. What is the Universe but an expression of Chronic Hunger. Time and Space ceaselessly copulate, devouring each other with admirable avidity. And from this perpetual fornication . . ."

"I do not think . . ." Edma began, but he cut in hastily:

"Odysseus, approaching the dry, herbaceous coasts of Arabia, cried: 'This air is ambrosial.' I, Madame, a sea dog in my own small way, say: This *broth* is ambrosial."

"Sea dog?" the Mother Superior wondered. "You are a sailor?"

"My boat is my mind," he explained, "my sea—the Universe."

"Ah!" she cried, impressed, and eagerly she sipped the pale brown wine that Emile had just then served her. The Exorcist held his glass beneath his nose and inhaled.

"A Jurançon!" he sighed, rolling the wine around and around in his swollen cheeks. "I cannot believe my good fortune! Emile—may I express my gratitude?"

"It is warming!" purred the Mother Superior, lapping at her wine with a very pink tongue.

"Illuminant!" said the Exorcist. "A toast! A toast to this garden"—this said with a broad sweep of the arm designating Edma's table—"of earthly delights!" They all drank; holding his glass out before him, the Exorcist continued:

"A legendary nectar. I recall that the king of Navarre chose it to baptize his puking, crapping brat, the future Henri IV (who paid with his life for his stubborn unwillingness to bow his head). A wine fit for kings; itself a king. I should say: queen. Admire her golden robe, caress her soft haunches, breathe her generous fragrance of cinnamon and clove. But what's this? A touch of acidity? The slut! She kisses, then bites; she's a pin concealed in her hem!" And turning to the blushing Mother Superior he lifted his glass and added:

"Be indulgent, blessèd creature—I live in dim rooms, my habitual sustenance watercress and water. . . ."

But the Mother Superior was not ruffled in the least. St.-Gemmes and her own torpid chambers seemed very far away indeed.

"Continue!" she pleaded. "So rarely in my stern universe of prayer and penance am I audience to such eloquent, uh, verbosity!"

Edma had served the hors d'oeuvres, and the Exorcist, engrossed by garnished cold meats, fell silent. A second bottle of Jurançon was fetched from the cellar and opened with a shy flourish by Emile.

The Mother Superior suddenly remembered Charlotte. "And the child?"

"Still convalescent, a recent relapse . . . perhaps later she will feel strong enough to come down," Edma said.

"Oh, I hope so!" exclaimed the Mother Superior. "But as she is not with us, we may speak of her with ease."

"Charlotte," said the Exorcist, surfacing from his plate, "like this red sausage"—and he held up a slice with his fork—"studded with fat, is pure poetry studded with numb spots. A passionate nature barded with ice and prodded incessantly by the Devil's own icepick."

"How dreadful!" exclaimed the Mother Superior.

"She's electric. I've touched her, I know," said the Exorcist. "A magnet placed between her thighs positively *wags*. Charlotte is precocious, pure, inspired—but savage! A changeling . . . tempestuous, quixotic—a dormant volcano . . ." and turning to Edma: "I hope that my portrait does not disturb you."

"Not at all!"

"It is a fine thing and noble, that you have taken an interest in her, *ma soeur*. She will be safe with you. Pearls must be kept from pigs."

"She *is* a pearl!" the Mother Superior agreed.

"She is the stuff saints are made of, *ma soeur!*"

"Yes! Yes! I believe she is!"

"I disagree!" Edma broke in, thrusting her fork into a pickle. "The child has the Devil in her!"

"As do we all, Madame. . . ." The Exorcist gazed deeply into the Mother Superior's pale eyes. "And that struggle for ascendancy and possession writhes within each heart as a worm in the belly of a hound. Temptation is everywhere, the fires of carnal lust glow in every alley. . . ."

"Ridiculous!" Edma snapped. "She is only ten years old!" And removing the dishes she went to fetch the duck. Emile shyly brought out a new bottle, an Algerian *Mascara*.

"Aha!" exclaimed the Exorcist when he saw the bottle. "The foul vampire phylloxera may have spat her pestilential spittle across the delicate damsel wines of France, but luckily for us all the obstinate *algériennes* have, thus far, survived the plague. She's a dusky wench," he added, licking his chops inquisitively, "her bones large and supple. She's plump and she's ready; she rolls over and asks only that we drink her. Perhaps she spreads her thighs too quickly, but then again, I am not a man to go to battle for a castle!"

The Mother Superior giggled, and hid her face with her veil.

"I see," he said to her, "that you are a woman of *spirit*." At this *bon mot* she laughed out loud.

"Monsieur Emile!" he cried. "It is time to open another bottle!" And having removed his left boot, he explored the Good Mother's ample skirts with his foot. Meeting with no resistance, he continued to probe, rooting at last between her conveniently spread thighs.

"Wine and flesh," he continued, "both gardens multiflorous. Each affords an insight into the joys reserved for the just—or so the Al Koran tells us. Heaven is no dry tundra pocked with liver-colored lichen, but a humid forest, generous to all the senses: sight, smell, sound—and touch. *In toto corde meo exquisiui te. . . .*" Taking aim, he thrust his big toe deep into the Mother Superior's well-oiled clockworks.

"Ah!" she cried.

"What's the matter?" asked Edma. "Choke on a bone?"

"I fear I've, uh, lost my ring!"

"I will look for your ring, my lady of the veils," said the Exorcist. "I'm sure to find it; it cannot be far."

"You've only just lost it?" asked Edma.

"Oh! No!" she sighed, visibly flummoxed. "I lost it before I came!" And she held his foot fast with her thighs.

"She lost it in the garden," said the Exorcist. "She lost it in the parsley." At this the Mother Superior giggled most suggestively.

"She lost it in Bluebeard's closet!" he added, giving a thrust; and once again she hid her face.

"Christ bade us drink his blood," said the Exorcist, raising his glass. "Drink, *ma soeur.* Is it not sweet?"

"Indeed it is sweet!" she breathed, slipping down in her chair. "Sweet! Sweet!"

"Then drink, *Rosa Mundi!*" and he gestured to Emile, who filled her glass.

"Madame Edma! You must drink too!" But Edma, confused by the direction the conversation had taken and feeling vaguely that she was the butt of some obscure and

unsavory joke, placed her hand over her glass and shouted:
"No more!" and sliced angrily into the gilded crust of the
roast duck. For a time they sat in silence, the Exorcist and
the Mother Superior each gnawing a wing. Emile clumsily
tackled his drumstick with knife and fork, spilling onions
and peas into his lap and onto the floor. Having returned
the peas to his plate from his pants, he got down on all fours
and crawled beneath the table to retrieve the rest. Once
there he stayed.

"Emile!" Edma whined, wringing her hands, her temper
worsening by the minute. "What are you doing under the
table, for God's sake?"

"I-I-I-" Emile began.

"Perhaps he's looking for something," said the Exorcist.

"P-P-P-Peas!" cried Emile.

"He is looking for Peace," the Exorcist explained. "Perhaps he has found it."

At this the Mother Superior frankly guffawed, a bawdy
outburst her veil could not mask. Merrily she giggled, her
breasts heaving beneath her wimple, her dimpled chin
aglow with grease.

Edma could stand it no longer.

"*Ma soeur!*" she cried, rising from her chair. "You behave
most unseemingly!"

"She can't hold her liquor," the Exorcist acknowledged.
Emile, still under the table, his face illuminated by the
Mother Superior's lighted lantern and captivated by the
agile play of the Exorcist's big toe, began to hum.

"Great Gods!" sang the Exorcist, recognizing the tune:

> "*Great Gods in Heaven I do beseech*
> *The power by some marvel:*
> *The bottom of a cunt always to breach*
> *The bottom of a bottle never to reach.*"

"I've had enough!" Edma cried. "You're all drunk!" The Mother Superior hiccuped and began to cry.

"God have Mercy!" she blubbered. Then all at once brightening, she dried her tears with her wimple and sang:

*"O Heavenly Father who keeps us from Sin,
How many angels can fit on a pin?"*

And from under the table Emile harped:

"H-H-H-How m-many many can fit on a pin?"

"I will fetch Charlotte!" Edma shouted above the clamor. It seemed the only thing she could do to sober the company.

Edma pushed Charlotte into the dining room. She stood there in her oddly stained dress, barefoot and red-eyed. Her face—yellow with powder—was streaked with tears and badly swollen; Edma had slapped her silly on the landing.

". . . the Universe is a clock and what is Time?" the Exorcist was raving to no one in particular. Indeed, Emile was nowhere to be seen, and the Mother Superior appeared to be fast asleep.

"Time is a mouth," he continued, "generative and autophagous."

"Wind the clock!" groaned the Good Mother with closed eyes.

"What is female flesh?" He ignored her and dipped his hand into the salad. "A vinegar-hole! A scrap of wilted lettuce!"

Edma coughed sharply. The Exorcist pulled his foot out from under the Mother Superior's skirts, and she, her face in her hands, slipped to the floor, sobbing. And as Edma pulled Charlotte from the room and pushed her back up the stairs, Emile appeared from under the table and attempted to dry the Mother Superior's tears with his soiled napkin.

She was wailing now, and it took an hour of cold compresses applied to her flaming brow to calm her. That night she slept in Edma's parlor; sober and penitent, she set off for St.-Gemmes the following day. *Dominus vobiscum. Ite, Missa est!*

CHAPTER
18

"I am . . . infatuated!" the Mother Superior admitted to the crucifix upon her return, her mind foggy with lust and self-loathing. "I am plagued with base longings of . . . voluptuous intent!

"Should I *fornicate?*" she asked, enthralled by the word she had said out loud, near mad with panic and fatigue. "Is it not conceivable," she reasoned, "that the consummation of Lust will prove Lust's cure? Lust, lust, *lust!*"

"The price of pleasure is *guilt,*" she distinctly heard the crucifix croak. "Guilt leads to . . . Humiliation!"

"Yes!" she agreed, nodding at the Christ's emaciated figure. "And Humiliation leads to God!" Her hunger justified, her excitement was boundless. She undressed and considered her sexual parts attentively.

"You are a garden!" she dreamed she heard the Exorcist's voice say. "Brambles and ripe fruit!"

"Am I in love?" she mused, terrified. Until now there had been only the Holy Ghost—who once in a dream had entered her womb. A white dove, plump and well-formed with a wet, pink beak, he had circled, circled, circled before settling down upon her—as on a nest—in a flash of radiance. She had arisen thrilled to the quick by the plodding of his little yellow feet, the hectic peck-peckings of his little beak, the beatings of his wings. . . . Were not these heavenly caresses enough to fill one woman's flesh, one woman's life? What more could the Exorcist bring her? She blushed as she thought of his member. Never had she seen a naked man; a loincloth draped her imagination, and his probing beneath the dinner table had remained mysterious, downright miraculous. How had he done it? With what? She imagined that, like the Devil's mythic prick, the Exorcist's was long and limber as an eel; that once unwound it had slid across the floor and up between her legs to explore her throbbing nakedness—so conveniently concealed beneath the dressed table.

In fever she rolled bare-skinned upon the cold floor, bruising her breasts and buttocks and back. Spreading her raised legs high in the air she raved:

"Come! Little Dove! Little beak! Prick me!"

But when the Holy Ghost, apparently peeved, rejected her, she plotted her next rendezvous with the Exorcist and the manner in which she would seduce him, polishing each particular in her mind until, rubbed to a smooth and throbbing shine, her daydream stood erect, perfect in every detail. His image consumed her: his emaciated body, those brooding, bloodshot eyes and crooked grin. She had seen so few men that his very maleness was admirable. So dark was he, so hard, so unlike the plump and spineless saints that hung from the chapel walls in staged poses of brooding melancholy! And so, even before the lovers' second meeting—a hasty embrace stolen among the blossoming cherry branches of Emile's garden (he had wounded her lip and mauled her tits), a spectacular shuffle and swift (O! Too swift!) penetration from behind (so that still she had not seen his prick!)—that most bestial of positions, he had gloated, as bleating he ripped her thighs and buttocks apart, her head pressed painfully against the unforgiving watering can in Emile's toolshed (as Emile smothered the eggs of his enemies in nicotine and Edma prepared the dinner: eel, the Exorcist had expressly asked for eel)—she was his.

"I am afraid of Evil," Charlotte confided to Emile one balmy spring morning in the garden. He pointed to the broken glass embedded in the high walls.

"N–N–N–No E–E–E–Evil here!" he soothed. "M–M–My garden is s–s–s–*safe!*"

But Charlotte knew that even in the safest of gardens dwells a snake.

CHAPTER
19

Came July, that month of feminine hysteria (the Exorcist), when the constellation of the dog rides the flanks of the sky and the pious fall to their knees in frenzies of self-disgust; Sirius, rising like Edma even before the sun, intimated that it was time she returned to Lourdes. As Charlotte was still too weak to travel, Edma went alone.

Charlotte and Emile were left by themselves. For the first time in many years Emile was free to wander where he would; a man of limited vision and desires, and with Charlotte's hand clasped well within his own, he trod up the hill to Madame Saignée's café, "The Poor Devil."

Charlotte took to the café at once. She admired the ceiling's plaster rosettes swelling like so many fringed nipples; she admired the "Turkish-style" porcelain shit-hole gaping at the room's far end behind a thick green door, and its mysterious window, no larger than a shoe box, that looked out upon a courtyard charged with empties and Madame Saignée's collection of alabaster dwarves, goddesses and geese.

Upon the oak counter by the entrance stood a redolent coffee machine and above it hung an enormous gold-and-black-framed mirror. Reflected therein from the opposite wall was a languorous, diaphanous nude, rising coyly from the limpid pool of a well-tended cow pasture. Three cows, arrested in their grazing, looked out across the grass upon her transparent, otherworldly yet voluptuous contours.

The waters had given birth to this happy marriage of flesh and spirit; she was both earthly *and* transcendent. The café's faithful called her Wet Winnie.

From the very first Charlotte chose to believe that her mother, that ill-fated sinner about whom Edma would speak, rarely, with lowered eyes and voice, had looked just like that. And ever after, when Charlotte thought of her mother, the image of Wet Winnie, rising like a moon from the cow pond, irresistibly came to mind. Until that moment, Charlotte's mother had been faceless, she'd had no body: she was spirit and she was bones and she was ashes. But now, comfortably installed at one of the old yellow tables, the engrossing histories of past and present lusts etched into its gleaming, mellow surface, a pale lemonade set before her in a thick, bubbled water glass, Charlotte sat undisturbed in the ecstatic contemplation of Wet Winnie, her mother.

If Charlotte took to the café, the café took to her. It was proclaimed by Père Poupine (who, to Emile's confusion, presented her with the largest snail anyone had ever seen) that Charlotte and her dancing rabbit would bring them all luck. Then he suggested that the café be called from then on "The Dancing Hare" instead of "The Poor Devil."

Charlotte was thin and odd in the peculiar frocks that Edma sewed and starched for her. But she had a shy grace, those wonderful changeling eyes (that Edma despised) and a nervous, soft pink mouth that, as Poupine sang in the late hours of that canicular night, long after Emile and Charlotte went home to bed:

> ". . . *was sliced just right*
> *a plum? Not quite—more like a berry.*
> *And when she bit her lower lip*
> *It reddened like a cherry.*"

And he added: "She'll bring the house down!"

CHAPTER
20

Several days after Edma's departure for Lourdes, savory days spent in the agreeable contemplation of La Saignée's forbidden fruit (tobacco, lemonade and Wet Winnie), yellow notices smelling smartly of fresh ink materialized beneath every door:

TONIGHT THE MISSING LINK
HAVING SWEPT WORLD CAPITOLS OFF THEIR FEET
MAKES A RARE APPEARANCE
AT THE FOOT OF THE CATHEDRAL
8 O'CLOCK

The Missing Link was an imposing black man named Samson La Liberté, a French Canadian who had made it to France billed as Satan the Fire-eater on Buffalo Bill's stunning European tour. Bill and Sam had come to fists over one Mademoiselle de Gaufrière, a high-titted, high-wire *artiste* Bill had uncovered under curious circumstances in a Parisian bordello. Sam had had no choice but to pull out his stake and go, but damned if that boy ain't downright charismatic (Annie Oakley) and without hesitation the lady had grabbed her ample bags and gone with him. In Lille they had hooked up with a crook who had been on the run with a suitcase of opium and orange india-rubber dildoes ever since the police had nearly nabbed him as he napped in the baroque hocus of a lavender bubble bath he could not afford—the bogus Dalai Lama, Bam-Bam Tantra, the Jewel-in-the-Lotus, Advayavajrasamgramaphone. Om!

That evening, everyone in the village who could walk on two legs or on four—the crowd that gathered included numerous dogs, three female goats and a mule—stood at the front steps of the church in vociferous admiration of a handsome bird's-egg blue cage made manifest as the locals had sat at home humbly partaking of the evening broth. (The Exorcist alone was missing, totally taken up as he was at that time by the thrilling possibilities of methane-powered windmills.)

A black curtain was hung around the cage, efficiently concealing the Missing Link from view. After fifteen minutes, the crowd pressed around impatiently and three young boys (whom Emile believed he recognized) went so far as to poke at the curtains with sticks. In response, a titanic roar sent them howling to their mother's familiarly mottled arms. And then from out the somber cathedral walked a graceful fat man in flowing saffron robes and polished skull, a third eye painted on his brow and smelling (as Madame Saignée whispered to La Fesse all too quickly, so giving herself away irretrievably) just like a fancy brothel!

"Peace and Fortune!" cried Ali Hassan Popa (for it was he), raising his hands above his head and spreading his rosy, ringed fingers in a salute he hoped was exotic. "Oh! Hum! My name is Seven Perfume and I come from the far and fragrant reaches of distant Tibet where I spent my childhood picking tea in the green gardens of Tsoin Tsoin and wandering the mossy mountains of Ur minding my yak. . . ."

"You sure not minding it *now!*" Père Poupine could not resist calling out rudely. "Where's the monster?"

"He's here!" Seven Perfume cried. "Here in this auspiciously hued and stalwart cage. To be disclosed to you presently, in truth: at any moment! But first a warning. You must all know that the Monster (as you, sir, accurately name him), known to the Western World as the Missing Link, who as you will see for yourselves is both a man *and* an animal *and* a recently proved relative of yours, sir (and I readily add of mine), is a ferocious creature of unbridled appetites, a man-eater of brontosaurian brutality and *abominable* inclinations. In my country we call him Yeti: The Abominable! He *can* (and he *has* and he'll *try!*) crush a man's skull-bone as if it were an egg! I've seen him tear off a man's ears, rip out his tongue and liver, play marbles with his eyeballs—his victim was an innocent shoe salesman from Nanaimo who, in the grips of unbridled curiosity (I learned too late the poor soul was astigmatic), got too close to the cage! So stand back, folks! *Don't approach the cage!* An infant Eskimo, a charming child of five, having thrust his little blubber-filled fist through the bars from pure unadulterated friendliness, was quartered before his mother's eyes and eaten alive to the everlasting horror of his entire family! I should add that I am the only human being he'll leave alone—indeed, I believe he *loves* me (if such a beast can be said to be capable of that sentiment) ever since the fatal day long ago when I found him weeping beside my modest twig dwelling and cured him of the toothache that had made his lonely life a Living Hell! But anyone else—I've *warned* you—he'll slice into steaks for Bluebeard! Hum!"

"This I gotta *see!*" cried Poupine, and the village brats, secure in maternal embraces and lusting for blood, cried out in high, tremulous voices:

"The Link! The Link! We want to see the Link!"

"Well then, pay up!" Seven Perfume shouted above the hullabaloo. "They paid gold nuggets in Nootka for a glimpse of my Yeti; for you sods I'm only asking ten sous!"

"How do we know he's authentic?" called Poupine, not overeager to give up hard cash on what might be better spent on hard liquor.

"You'll know just as soon as you see him!" Seven Perfume assured him. Clapping his hands, he called out: "Gaufrette!"

Mademoiselle de Gaufrière, who'd been standing just behind the cathedral doors all this time in her little white buckskins, bodice and boots, swayed forth, bosom and hair piled high, to take up the collection. One look at her caused Poupine to cry: "Countrymen, this *is* authentic!" And when she approached him: "You want my money, Mam'zelle, Hell! Take my *life!*"

Mademoiselle de Gaufrière took his knotty red face between her cool hands and, kissing him firmly on his hot, dry lips, silenced him for the rest of the night. Once she'd made the rounds, tucking each coin into the little leather purse that dangled between the trembling moons of her perfect breasts, Seven Perfume parted the curtains to reveal a roaring near-naked colossus, glistening like coal rubbed in oil, his head and chest hair stained bright orange, his genitals straining impressively within a little lion-fur loincloth that caused La Fesse to mutter in admiration:

"He's nothing missing as far as I can see!"

The cage was too small for him; he had to stoop and with his broad, muscular back bent and massive, growling head thrust forward, he looked wonderfully ferocious. As one man the crowd gasped and stepped back. Charlotte took Emile's hand and stared transfixed; she knew she was breathing the same air as a cannibal!

Never had anyone seen a black man, nor any man, so exposed. Indeed the hyperbolical loincloth did not conceal the beauties that nested within, but by molding them so extravagantly, both glutted and surpassed the imagination. The "sods" (as Seven Perfume dared call them) did not doubt that they were witness to a phenomenon eolithic; a solid gold link with the obscure and stormy origins of mankind, the living proof of the cataclysmic theory of planetary history then at the apex of fashion. The monster roared and the stars spun free from their orbits to smash together in blinding conflagration. He rolled his eyes and the seas parted. He rocked his cage (how flimsy it seemed now, ready to splinter into a thousand brittle fragments!) and comets tore into the tranquil summer sky above their heads. When he drummed upon his chest men's hearts failed; when he scratched his crotch, feminine hearts faltered.

"Can you argue authenticity now?" Seven Perfume cried.

"This is the genuine article! An unbridled force of nature! Does blood flow through these veins or fire? Do tears flow from these eyes or lava? Is he flesh? Or is he the materialization of evil?" Dogs barked: *Get back! Back! Back!,* the goats took to their heels, the mule brayed and defecated profusely; women wept and children begged to be taken home. The smell of sulphur permeated the air.

"And yet!" Seven Perfume cried as the Missing Link, looking all at once both sleepy and peaceful, lowered himself to the floor of the cage. "When I nursed his wound he was all tenderness, as gentle as a lamb, as trusting as a virgin." The Missing Link had rolled himself into a fetal position. He appeared to be asleep. Madame Saignée and La Fesse both felt a definite stirring of latent maternal instinct.

"Poor, lonely Yeti . . ." Seven Perfume sighed, slowly closing the curtain. "He sleeps now, as will you all, safe in the knowledge that his sleep is deep and his cage is solid. And he who sleeps, dreams. My Yeti dreams of Tibet, his beloved homeland, the land of the lotus and the sacred seed . . ." and spreading out his arms he added: "*Om!*"

"*Ommm!*" Emile rolled the word on his tongue.

The crowd slowly dispersed, relieved that it was over, yet wistful. Aged couples, their eyes bright with freshly stirred embers, walked off arm in arm to the humid privacies of the marriage bed.

"*B-b-b-beautiful!*" Emile gasped. "L-l-like G-G-God!" And he stood before the cage, Charlotte at his side, long after everyone else had gone home. Seven Perfume feared that he had been recognized and whispered nervously into de Gaufrière's mother-of-pearl ear before eclipsing for the night. She gyrated over to Emile and patting Charlotte on the head said:

"You just wait here, *chérie,* I've a little business to do with the gentleman." And taking Emile by the hand, she led him into the dark church.

Charlotte sat down on the church steps for what seemed a very long time and warily watched the cage. Suddenly the curtain parted and the Missing Link stepped down into the street.

"You still here?" he said amiably.

"You *t-talk?*" Charlotte whispered, too frightened to run.

"I talk!" he guffawed. He laughed so hard that he began to cry, and Charlotte was relieved to see that his tears were like her own.

"What you waiting for?" he said at last.

"My un-eu-eu-le."

"Your uneule?"

"My, uh, uh, aunt's 'usband."

"Your uncle! He visiting with Gaufrette?"

"Uh. 'ess."

"What's wrong with your voice?"

"I . . . uh, ate eu-eu 'lass."

"You ate what? What was that you ate?"

"Eu-eu 'lass. Eu-eu G! Lass!"

"Glass? You're saying you ate *glass?*" Charlotte nodded. "What in the name of Christ you do *that* for?"

Charlotte thought it over. Then she pointed to the Stain.

"*Tabernac!* You're telling me you ate *glass* because of that little patch of brown you've got on your face?" Charlotte nodded. "Mam'zelle, I'm brown all over and I never ate no glass! I've eaten fire," he added after a moment's reflection, "but, Hell, I got *paid* for that."

Before they could talk more, Emile stumbled out of the church buttoning his trousers and grinning from ear to ear.

"I've had a nice little conversation with your niece here," Sam La Liberté said, offering Emile his hand. Emile's jaw dropped.

"Y–y–y–you t–t–t–*talk?*" he said.

The Exorcist pulled at the front doorbell impatiently. Now that Edma had gone to Lourdes, he wanted to spend some time alone with Charlotte, to touch her, to place a hand upon the soft sphere of her childish knee, to caress the Stain and feel its velvety fire beneath his fingers. During her convalescence he had often fondled her knee, investigated the blind eye of her perfumed navel with a moist forefinger, pursued more intimately still as she slept and dreamed her little girl's startling dreams. . . .

The kitchen door was locked, the grounds deserted, and he roamed the garden like a lost dog. The rabbit hutches were nearly all empty; he supposed that Edma had slaughtered and bottled the creatures before leaving and he imagined that there must have been a great deal of gore.

The child brides of Bengal, he mused, are spattered with the blood of roosters to resemble trophies of war; the nubile nymphets of Nubia are abandoned in the badlands where their flesh is seasoned for love by the bites of beasts, venomous brambles and thorns. . . .

The Exorcist approached the toolshed. It was unlocked. Walking stealthily, he peered about. He saw jars of nails, seeds, copper sulphate and nicotine; watering cans, rakes and hoes leaned against the walls, crayfish traps hung from the rafters and a large pair of rubber boots occupied the only chair. On the table—partially concealed beneath a clutter of seed catalogues, garden manuals and rags—he saw an imposing black leather box.

The Exorcist had discovered Emile's knives.

Like Roman wedding rings and the chains of slaves, they were made of iron. . . . But so finely polished, there was not one speck of rust to be seen on any blade.

Such a knife, he thought with excitement, raising one into the air, could slice the knot that binds the Spirit to the Body in a wink! And he pressed it tenderly against his lower belly—beneath the heavy, soiled cloak he wore no matter the weather—and meditated upon the Fragility of Flesh:

How many years it takes to form a man, and yet! How easily is a man undone. Did that not prove, once again, that Satan's is the greater Power?

That night as Charlotte slept, Emile brought the box of knives into the kitchen. He cleared a place for it on the table and sat down and embraced it, his cheek resting on the smooth leather. For a time he sat, quiet and content, the box filling his heart and his arms like a lover.

"A-a-ah!" he breathed, dreaming of Mademoiselle de Gaufrière's lips. And intimately he fiddled with the hinges.

Gently, Emile opened the lid and with tears in his eyes admired the treasures spread before him. Then one by one, he fondled the knives and lay them down upon the blue cloth in neat rows, just as he might have a garden. He regretted that they could not be planted, grow roots and leaves, bear fruit. . . .

"S-s-s-o, so beautiful!" He sighed. "B-but . . ." he wondered, his heart constricting—Gilles de Rais was missing.

CHAPTER
21

Edma had packed a voluminous luncheon basket and yet all day went hungry, unable to eat in public, before strangers, as if mastication were as much a sin as fornication. She was sweltering in her black bombazine dress and it took her hours to admit to herself (and the other passengers) that she must relieve her bladder in the evil-smelling WC down a screaming hole—like an old codger's toothless mouth—above the tracks. My Lord, she peed into open air upon uncovered ground! She feared she would pay for her impropriety.

Her carriage, like the entire train, was packed with pilgrims on their way to Lourdes, and Edma feared contamination; it resounded with a party of tubercular orphans spitting out scraps of their tormented lives into filthy handkerchiefs. Beside her sat a woman oozing pus, and a man (presumably her husband—the couple held hands) nurturing a fantastic goiter from which Edma had difficulty keeping her eyes. It was held in place by a curious one-cupped brassiere-like affair. In front of her sat an individual whose hair had been replaced by scabs, and an elderly gentleman without arms. Edma wondered if during her short pilgrimage a miracle would take place. And, if so, would one of these persons be cured? The problem of cure haunted Edma. It was evident that God made men sick to punish them. Having gone through all the trouble of riddling his depraved subjects with multitudinous ills, it seemed therefore an odious waste of God's precious energies to then take it upon Himself to cure what He had provoked. God's ways are mysterious, she reminded herself, yawning.

And when she kneeled before Our Lady of Lourdes' clammy grotto, should she pray for salvation, or should she pray to be absolved of those disgraceful warts on her feet once and for all? No one would see her feet until her death when they would be visible to whomever would come to wash them. Edma hoped it would not be Charlotte. (One look at my feet, Edma considered, stupid with approaching sleep, and I shall lose all my authority!) The train rocked along, hour after hour, and Edma slept, dreaming that she sped down a river of pus in a stiff wicker basket that was far too small for her and her belongings and in grave danger of spilling its contents at any moment. She saw nothing of the mountains, spectacular gorges and river-studded valleys for which the majestic countryside she crossed was so famous. When she awoke it was already dark; other passengers had begun to unwrap greasy provisions from oily hampers; but Edma still refused to partake of food. When she arrived at Lourdes at last, after fourteen hours in the train, she was famished, sooty and ill-tempered. Fortunately the Immaculate Conception was still serving the evening meal and Edma, after staring ferociously at the other clients, then for the greater part finishing their cheese, sawed her way through a slippery slice of veal, and noticed to her infinite disgust a very small spot of what could only be blood on the edge of the tablecloth. Shuddering, she supposed that a tubercular person had passed that way earlier and had had the impertinence to cough. She hoped it had not been her waiter.

The following day, Edma took to her knees. She and over one thousand people, excepting those on wheelchairs or crutches or, for that matter, without knees (war veterans mostly, and one poor devil in the final stages of leprosy), kneed their way from the Paths of Hope and Charity to the Road of Chastity, around the Hemicycle of the Rosary, into a cathedral that stank of suppurated flesh; then down and around the Hemicycle once again, across the Court of Quiet to the Grotto of Massabielle where the pubescent Bernadette had seen the Virgin Mary eighteen times to the wails of wind instruments and the clatter of hail, of crystal in spontaneous generation, the sobs of inquisitive angels, the lunatic chirpings of birds and the giddy flailings of her own heart. And each time she had stood transfixed within a wheel of fire that turned the very marrow of her fragile bones into (as she had explained to her terrified mother) weak broth.

The multitude wept and sang as it painfully approached the grotto: *We are walking towards you, Lord!* But, in truth, nobody was walking. They were all of them crawling or sliding, although some of them hobbled. From the grotto's dripping walls, like Transylvanian insects of prey, numerous black crutches were hanging—proof that some fortunate creatures, having made the trip as four-legged animals, had, like the frisky young pigs of nursery rhymes, wee-weed all the way home upon two.

Edma was satisfied only once her knees had begun to bleed. Her arms stretched out on either side of her body, she prayed—as rigid as the Cross itself—motionless but for her lips and the fingers of her right hand feeling up the black beads of her rosary. She knew that here a blind boy, the retinas of both eyes having peeled away like old paint, had seen again. That an illiterate, comatose eleven-year-old girl had risen from her granny's lap to sing the *Song of Solomon* in papal Latin. That a man swathed in thick scales had shed this disgrace with the ease of a molting snake.

"Remove the warts!" Edma prayed. "Remove Charlotte's Stain," she added, "if you think the child *worthy*."

That night Edma took a bath. Her knees were stiff and burned in the hot water. And if the warts still plagued her feet, she knew from her pain that she, at least, was worthy of salvation.

"I'm bleeding for you, Lord!" she needled, soaping her withered teats.

Each day Edma traced the same itinerary until the flesh of her knees was mashed to jelly. By the time she was ready to go home, she could stand only with the help of a cane she had bought from one of the numerous souvenir shops.

The scabs will be very impressive, she thought on the train. When they drop off, I'll take care to save them. . . .

CHAPTER

22

That summer Emile gave Charlotte a velocipede. He disen-
tangled it from the toolshed—rusty and tasselated with
webs and the egg-sacs of spiders—and in an explosion of
inspired tenderness hammered it back into a recognizable
shape. It had an iron body and iron wheels, it was willful
and unwieldy—but Charlotte set about at once to master it.
Though she was terrified at first, it was above all curiosity
that swept her along and not the pungent taste of freedom.
But the bicycle gave her wings and within a few passionate
days she learned to use them, and pedaled forth to discover
the country of Grace she had perceived in the foxed surface
of Madame Saignée's mirror—winking seductively from
behind Wet Winnie's golden hair.

Throughout the warm, shining days of August, Charlotte
explored the dusty roads that led away from La Folie. She
spent long, delicious hours dreaming in the grass beside
the region's desolate pride—that great, granite menhir in
whose shadow she had been conceived, the Devil's Finger.
The rambles made her strong and limber and within a week
she had come to scale that finger; straddled on its mossy
summit she drank in the wind, dizzy with the promise of
her new-found autonomy.

In the beginning she dared ride only to the edge of the
village; she would stop at the greengrocery to catch her
breath and to gaze into the brightly shifting waters of green

glass before returning dutifully home. But Edma was preoc-
cupied and glad to have her out of the way. And so she
wandered further each day, past the church, the cemetery,
past the fountain where the brawny laundresses washed the
scrawls of conception, death and infidelity from the linens,
beating them against the smooth, worn stones as they joked
and gossiped; past the summer gardens, bright and dreamy
with phlox, hortensia and violet lupine; past the windmills
and the ripening vines and even past the fields of wheat into
the deep, lush regions of pasture land where every cow
pond brought to mind Wet Winnie.

In those days the ditches swarmed with fat crayfish and
when by chance Charlotte met Père Poupine, he offered
to share a late afternoon's feast of Sweet Annies—steamed
and spiced only with wild shallot and amity. Fleas at his feet
and a mess of crayfish piled high in a metal washbasin that
Edma would surely have recognized for the deep dent in
its side, Père Poupine told her all he knew (and was there
anything he did not know?) about life, love, the seasons and
dogs.

". . . Human love leads to treason and human friendship
to deception. But never underestimate a companion like
Fleas. He's independent, a fine hunter, stays only because
he enjoys my companionship and because he knows I value
his—don't you, now?" In answer, Fleas lay his head on
Poupine's knee.

"Oo don't trust people?" asked Charlotte, a little uneasy.

"I trust Fleas," Poupine said, worrying the dog's silky
ears. "And . . . I trust Archange Poupine!" And when Charlotte looked crestfallen, he threw her a pilfered vineyard
peach, patted her on the cheek and laughing said: "And
you, Dancing Rabbit!"

That summer Poupine taught Charlotte some songs.
Among them:

Lazy live long,
Miser can't sleep.
Bird on the wing—
Be damned if he don't sing!

And he often repeated: Overwork is a vi-o-lation of common sense!

"Today, like tomorrow, I run with Fleas in the woods—on the lookout for pheasant and mushrooms. Or wade in the clear water up to my belly catching trout." He chuckles to himself. "Or mucking after duck—hé! Think of it, Fleas! Mucking after duck!" Fleas jumps up and starts to whine, ready to start out at once. "Or crawling around on my knees after star jelly (must have rain first for *that,* yes—need rain, three days rain . . .)." He seems to be dreaming.

"Star jelly?"

"Moon-spit! Never seen it? Never seen Moon-spit? Hé! Hé! You've got the eyes, daughter! Next time it rains a good rain, take a look around on the ground. You'll see it; truly, it shines like an eye. Good for the lungs." He coughs. "*De Dieu!*"

"The moon *spits?*"

"Well, in truth now, Charlotte, it sheds a little—sheds a little, falls through the sky and then: *plop!* Aha! Moon-stuff!"

"Tell me about the moon." She has come close to him, and she has taken Fleas into her arms.

"Hah! I'll tell you—there are people up there, lots of them, Mam'zelles, even like yourself! I've seen them!" He laughs. "Name of God, they've wings like bats—"

"Angels!"

"Poo, not angels! Phooey!" He frowns. "I said *people.* People with wings like bats. I've seen 'em, flying like ducks over those big moony lakes."

"Lakes of water?"

"Hé, hé, hé! Lakes of *wine!*"

She is thoughtful. "You lie around like that on the euh-g-ground after dark watching the moon and not afraid?"

"Afraid of *what*, Rabbit?"

"Wolves! Aunt says: After dark the wolves leap from the maw of Hell with hate in their hearts!"

"Hé! I'd trust a wolf faster than your Aunt Edma! Wolves aren't like men, Rabbit. It's just famine makes them cruel and that's the truth. I've known wolves to devour a melon patch and leave the sleeping baby in his crib to his dreams. Yes. Now I'll tell you . . ." and he lowered his voice. "The roots of all things whisper together under the earth. The wolves know far more about the world (Oh, they *know* things!) than most people—living among the roots as they do. I've a friend, a she-wolf, just had four pups last spring—she brought them over one day while I was roasting some fish on the fire. 'Archange,' she says, 'I want to introduce you to my sons!' "

"Ooh! What were they called?"

"Let's see, hah! They was called, hum, *Frrrrou.*"

"Frrrrou?"

"Grrrrou!"

"Grrrrou!"

"And, uh, Napoleon. And, uh, let's see, Casimir!"

"Casimir!" Charlotte rocks with laughter. "Casimir?"

"Well," he admits, "was more like, ha! *Casimmmrrraa!*"

"O, Archange!" Charlotte cries, and she hugs his knees, utterly happy.

Poupine knew the names of all the wildflowers of the woods, roadsides and meadows: griffin's foot and serpent's pink; great lightning (a cure for warts) and yellow hen's foot, which looked just like its name; foxtail, wall-pepper, goat's beard (and goat's stench!). Dead man's grass made excellent tea and she must never, never sleep in viper weed!

And *this,* my little beauty, is Venus's mirror . . . a bouquet for her, scarlet and fragrant.

He told her that wizards are born with their hats on; that a red moon in the west means wind; he told her about the drinking man who rang a loud bell to keep from swallowing the Devil. . . .

"What happened?"

"The Devil slipped in his mouth when he was sleeping!"

He told her the story of the jealous crow who stole a wedding ring; the story of the angry toad who lived with her daughter-in-law in a crypt, and who was so proud, and who swelled to such proportions, that she toppled a famous cathedral to the ground. And he told her that the Devil's Finger was in truth a pebble that Gargantua the giant had found once, long ago, in his shoe. . . .

"I know something too!" Charlotte said. "Mary went to Heaven without dying!" To this Poupine replied:

"Some people are monkeys!" He cuffed her ear gently. "And monkeys, Charlotte, being people, should not be kept in cages."

One day, near the summer's end, Poupine said:

"I knew your mother." Charlotte, her mouth full of blackberries, gasped and nearly choked.

"My *mother!*"

"A damned pretty woman. However, you look like your father. He was a damned good-looking man!"

"You knew my parents! What were they like?" Charlotte jumped to her feet and tugged at her dress nervously. "You see," she added, "*she* won't tell me anything."

"Well," said Poupine, "you know that your mother died in childbirth." Charlotte nodded. "And your father drank like a fish; he drank more than any man I'll ever know, he drank even more than me! He drank as if his life depended on drinking, *nom di Dieu!* I never once saw him sober, although I often saw him hung over. Now you'll admit that's not the kind of man your Aunt Edma's going to talk about!" and he chuckled.

"Is . . . he . . . dead?" It had taken all her courage to ask. Often she had wondered why her father had never come for her. Once, when very little, she had asked Edma if one day he would. Edma had said:

"You *have* no father!"

Poupine answered her question:

"No man can drink like your father and live." He snorted and reached down between his legs for his own bottle. "How's that uncle of yours?" he asked, dropping the subject, which threatened to submerge them both. Charlotte was thinking: Did my mother really look like Wet Winnie? But she did not dare ask.

"He's all right," she said. "He likes vegetables better than people."

"I like your uncle," said Poupine. "He's a fine species of human bean." This was just the sort of thing that usually made Charlotte laugh, but talk of her parents had sobered her; she was thinking of them with such intensity that had Poupine kept silent, she might have conjured them both up from the clay at her feet.

"What's going to become of you, Rabbit, when I'm gone and you no more a seedling but a full-grown flower? Ever think about that? Ever think about what you want to *be?*" Charlotte loved and trusted Poupine, but could she tell him?

"I want," she hesitated, "I want," she whispered, "I want . . . I want to be a *saint.*"

"I'll be damned!" He took a long drink from his bottle. Charlotte stood now, bending over him, and gave him a quick kiss on his prickly jaw. Then she picked up her bicycle and as she rode away over the uneven ground, Poupine rose awkwardly to his feet and shouted after her:

"Hé! Hé! That's a fool thing! Hé! Why, that's damned *crazy!*"

On her way back to La Folie, Charlotte saw the Téton twins. They were hanging over the road from the branch of a large walnut tree. Both were wearing wooden shoes, torn knickers and—despite the warm weather—flat wool caps. They also wore large grins; one grin disclosed a chipped front tooth. For a good minute, Charlotte and the twins stared at each other. It was Charlotte who first said:

"Hullo."

"Quihuitl!" said Gontran.

"Quihuitl!" Gaston echoed.

"K-Qui-huitl!" Charlotte said. The nourishing summer had almost healed her voice. The twins, obviously pleased, beamed down at her like two identical men-in-the-moon (one with a chipped tooth). They hung from their branch silently smiling and stared at her with great, round eyes until she felt uncomfortable.

"Uh. Do you want to *play?*" she asked.

"Ptooh!" Charlotte jumped back. The twins had spat at the ground simultaneously and were shaking their heads emphatically from side to side. Their eyes had narrowed.

"Well," Charlotte said, piqued, "well then. Good-bye."

"Yax snatch!" Gontran corrected her.

"Yax snatch," said Charlotte, a bit weary; and then, suddenly inspired, she added:

"Kristmax!"

But it was at once apparent that she had gone too far. For suddenly, and as one man, the twins stuck out their very red tongues and with rude, guttural noises, wagged them at her. Charlotte gasped.

"Some people!" she shouted, blushing and close to tears as she climbed back on her bicycle, "some people are . . . monkeys!"

CHAPTER

23

"The Envoys of Heaven are always vegetarian," said the Mother Superior as she held Charlotte's hand firmly in her own. Edma was boiling bones, and the kitchen—already sweltering in the heat of midsummer—was filled with steam. Pacing the room and perspiring in his shiny black suit, the Exorcist added:

"Cucumbers are gorged with light. . . ."

"God is contained in plants," the Mother Superior cut in eagerly. "When we eat plants, we eat Him." As Charlotte's mouth fell open in confusion, the Exorcist explained:

"In the beginning, the demons of the lower regions, chained to the Cogs of Time and sickened by the rotations of the zodiac, aborted, thus occasioning the World and dissipating the Light of God throughout the plant and animal kingdoms. Animals eat plants and as the human soul loses more spiritual energy assimilating this corrupted light than it receives. . . ."

"The Envoys of Heaven are always vegetarian!" The Mother Superior sat back triumphantly. And she summed up the afternoon's lesson with the suggestion that as cooking destroys the luminosity of plants, Charlotte had better eat her cucumbers raw.

"What about crayfish?" Charlotte asked.

"What *about* crayfish?" The Mother Superior was confused.

"Are . . . do . . . are they light? Or dark?" The Mother Superior looked helplessly at the Exorcist. So far her indoctrination had not broached the subject of crustacea.

"Crayfish, crabs and so forth," he said, searching his memory, "are, as I recall, very dark, very dark indeed."

Charlotte had one more question.

"Euh. Euh. . . . What are the Téton twins?"

"Monsters!" he replied. "Monstrosity squared! Monstrous to have twinned in the womb! Monstrous to have—despite this initial monstrosity—developed a deceptive *normality!* Oh, they are *dark!* In some countries twins are tortured, put to death!"

"Oh! *Why?*" Charlotte was terrified.

"To calm the fevers of those mortals who have no double to protect them from the Evil Eye! In a curious way they are your brothers . . . born the same day. Now *that* was a season of miracles!" And reaching for her face, he traced the Stain with a greasy finger. Charlotte suppressed the desire to bite him.

From the kitchen window, Edma looked on as the Exorcist and the Mother Superior continued to talk alone together in the garden. With bowed head and bright eyes, the Mother Superior listened attentively to the heretical creed of Mani.

"Sexuality," said the Exorcist (Edma was eavesdropping), "has its roots in every garden. . . ."

"As does Nostalgia," the Mother Superior whispered, inspired, "for an earlier epoch when Matter was shorn of Risk."

"Matter," the Exorcist reprimanded, "*is* Risk."

Meanwhile Charlotte fidgeted in her chair, lifted crumbs from the cracks in the kitchen table with a hairpin and picked her nose.

"Idle fingers do the Devil's work!" Edma snapped. "Go

and fetch your sewing!"

Charlotte went to her room for the underthings she was in the process of embroidering with her initials. As she sewed by the light of the open door she deliberated upon the afternoon's lesson. It occurred to her that a Truly Spiritual Person must one day cease to consume matter—both animal *and* vegetable—entirely. Considering her noble and bitter destiny, she was moved to tears.

"Stop that!" Edma shouted from the sink and before Charlotte could hedge Edma had grabbed her by the shoulders and was shaking her violently. "Or I'll give you something to squeal about!" She slapped Charlotte hard across the mouth. Charlotte gathered up her sewing and ran howling up the stairs to her room.

Edma removed the bones from the pan and left them to cool beside the open window. Later she would take them outside to dry and bleach in the sun beside the rake, prepared to smash in the skulls of vagrant cats. The bones were the primary matter for a project Edma had hatched on the train home: the construction of an exact replica of the Basilica of Lourdes. Edma firmly believed that to secure Grace she must leave something of Beauty behind her; that such a gesture would assure her a peaceful afterlife. Unlike the banal expressions of religious piety conceived of matchsticks, Edma's basilica would have the appearance of ivory and she would not have spent a single *sou!* Not only had the Mother Superior given her wholehearted approval, she had told the convent cook to keep all leftover bones aside for Edma.

Very little meat was prepared at St.-Gemmes—the girls survived for the most part on porridge. But a boiled rooster dinner for one hundred and twenty meant at least as many bones—picked very clean.

The convent cook—Sorberina Sopapo—was a miserable wench of twenty who, having no place of her own, slept on the convent kitchen table. She smelled of the onion and vegetable scraps which clung to the elbows of her indissoluble jersey. The Good Mother had come upon her in the forest, pregnant and kicking and hanging by the neck from a rope she had herself knotted inadequately. Her baby, born shortly after the Good Mother had cut Sorberina down, was kept in an apple basket beside the wood stove.

The only female survivor in a family of twenty, Sorberina had been persistently raped and beaten by her father and fifteen brothers. They had also knocked in most of her teeth. Speech was a humiliation she'd had no choice but to relinquish. It had not been easy to get her story, but once her tongue had come untied, she had talked for over five hours without once stopping to catch her breath and before her fractured mouth had shut again (and apparently forever) a sordid fresco smeared with blood, sperm and tears had come to light.

The Mother Superior took Sorberina under her wing. As luck would have it, the convent cook, an oily, hypocritical Breton, had been caught trussing a novitiate behind a slop pail and had been sent packing the very morning of Sorberina's aborted suicide. The Mother Superior simply inferred that the poor creature was Heaven-sent. Sorberina's cooking was almost palatable and that was more than was called for, although she occasionally mistook the salt for the sugar. Her only weakness was an exaggerated fondness for jam and for weeping. Had her nose been several centimeters shorter and her expression a trifle more lively, she might have been called passably pretty. However, there was something definitely amiss with little Caramelito who, if he never cried, never laughed either. And he slept with his eyes open.

Sorberina carried the bones to Edma, who took a liking to her homely face and paid for her services with string and spoonfuls of jam. Sorberina suffered terribly when the bone pail remained empty. A realist, she knew that bones from the neglected areas of the cemetery could be had for the asking and of finer quality than those rubbery bits she gleaned, so rarely, from the dinner scraps. Shortly after, she appeared at the door with a pail of human ribs and a piece of pelvis that the undertaker, a lean and hungry youth with vegetation on his hands and unusually prominent eyes, had obligingly unearthed for her with his shovel. Edma was scandalized, called Sorberina a witch and a heretic and from then on treated her with severity, paying her for her trouble with cruel cuffs on the ears. And Sorberina, having lost the estimation of a rare human being who had shown her kindness, withdrew further into herself, her only solace pilfered jam, thoughts of suicide and her silent son whom she cared for with obsessive solicitude, dipping her nipples in powdered sugar prior to each feeding. If Caramelito made no noises of contentment when he fed, neither did he complain, but stared fixedly at the little brown mole that grew beside his mother's left tit or the moon-shaped liver spot that rode above her right.

Charlotte entered St.-Gemmes in September 1884, one month before her eleventh birthday, with a new cardboard suitcase and a prayerbook of the cheapest sort. She was given a bed, a dented pewter cup with a flaming heart etched into it with acid, a fork and a spoon, a black alpaca dress and one month's allowance of toilet paper—newspaper cut into equilateral triangles and held together with string.

From the moment she perceived the grim structure—its sunken roof and crumbling foundations, its listing towers and bricked-up windows, the doleful wastes of its front courtyard, the lamentable state of its great, ominous gates and their filthy balls of brass—she knew that St.-Gemmes was nothing like what the Mother Superior had led her to believe. She had dreamed a fairy palace and now Edma marched her down the road towards the grimacing visage of a vast, decaying ruin, worried by wind, riddled by rain, and above all pocked by the acid bite of saltpeter that had gouged gaping wounds an arm's length deep into the foundations, and crusted the mottled façade with flaking black scales. It was a miracle that St.-Gemmes stood upright, when to all appearances a sneeze should have sent it thundering to the ground. To complete this vision of desolation, the abandoned vineyards stretching to the horizon on all sides were blasted by phylloxera.

With sudden illumination, Charlotte understood and was humbled. How childish she had been! She was not yet worthy of the St.-Gemmes of her dreams . . . the road to Him was cold and narrow. *I must prove myself!* she thought, and with a worried look, she bit her lower lip.

"This is it," Edma barked, anxious to start the long walk home. The Mother Superior spotted them and crossed the busy courtyard to pull open the screaming gate. She greeted Edma and to Charlotte said:

"Welcome to the House of Merciful Agony! It is *your* house now!" Having taken leave of Edma, she whispered into Charlotte's ear: "Once you are settled in, I'll invite you to my rooms and show you some of my *very* curious treasures!" And she led her to a group of newcomers like herself who were being pushed and prodded into a very straight line by a fiercely funereal nun.

"She's off my hands at last!" Edma muttered as she trotted on back to La Folie. She stopped at the Exorcist's house before going home. She found him sprawling on the kitchen floor and staring at a "self-perpetuating and aqueous" chess set he had bought that morning from an opulent Ali Hassan Popa dressed in stars and carrying a celestial globe. As the chessmen were alive and incredibly small, the Exorcist was attempting to manipulate them with the help of a hand-glass and a very long, thin needle.

". . . One-celled animals," he explained, "stained in lively colors." He was staring fixedly into a dish the size of a stamp. "Would you like to play a game? I've another glass."

"I hate games," said Edma. "Especially ones I can't see. I have come to say that I've taken her to St.-Gemmes. She is in the Mother Superior's hands now."

"And mine! Ever mine!" he corrected her. "I have this!" And he took a filthy object out of his pocket, made of hair, milk teeth, clock springs, nail parings and what appeared to be bits of intimate linen.

CHAPTER
24

Sister Malicia—a cadaverous creature as human as a broom handle, her arms knotted across her flat chest to protect the inverted nipples that dented the flesh like the cruel traces of tacks, her pale blue eyes lying loosely in their sockets like faded minerals in sagging boxes—carried her lovelessness with majesty. With a voice tortured by a tight larynx into the nightmarish urgencies of a twisted bassoon, she gave the newcomers a lecture in good conduct and humble obedience eloquently illustrated by a smooth paddle, a cat 'o nine and a bouquet of fresh nettles that she had herself picked barehanded. This interview was concluded by an ominous quote from Bernadette Soubirous, who had succumbed not long before to tuberculosis of the marrow (and not, as was generally supposed, to a malignant tumor that had for years squatted tenaciously upon her knee): "The more I am crucified, the greater will be my pleasure." The spectacle of Sister Malicia's martyred right hand impressed them for the nettles had raised red welts upon the palm, welts not unlike those that would be raised, only more so, upon the noviitiates' creamy buttocks, or so she was pleased to inform them, in dry, clerical tones, should they, but for an instant, step from the path of righteousness and indulge, however fleetingly, in frivolity.

"I do not know the meaning of the word *mercy*," Sister Malicia said, clutching herself tightly, her emotions betrayed by the beaded thread of saliva that bridged her open lips. "God knows His own; I do not. Knowledge is God's art and His Reason to Be. I know only the Rules. And if it is God's pleasure to Damn or to Grace, it is my pleasure, in this life, to Damn or to Grace in His name. My name is Sister Malicia and I expect you will never forget it. And now!" she added, unbinding her arms and raising them energetically into the air. "Down on your knees, all of you! Heads bowed! To the ground! And repeat after me:

"*Miserere nostri.* It means 'pity us.' You will *need* God's pity," she roared, strutting before the row of prostrate figures and pushing Charlotte's white face to the floor with her hand, ". . . you will *need* God's pity, for I have *none!*" And she wrapped her arms about herself as if to keep from unwinding like a top and permuting into a genie, a cyclone or worse. "Now! Stand! File out! To your dormitory! And silence! *Perfect silence!*"

Charlotte's "keeper" was waiting for them in the hall. Her name was Sister Purissima. She had a clubfoot but although she walked like a listing ship, lurching and gliding, Charlotte was impressed at once by the sweetness of her expression. Her face was a perfect oval, like an egg, and her eyes were flooded with a liquid brown like melted chocolate. Despite her deformity she had extraordinary dignity and Charlotte's heart went out to her at once. Sister Purissima could not have been more than sixteen.

"There are no foxes here, no birds, no red poppies, no wild roses, nor fields of wheat," said Sister Purissima as the girls readied themselves for bed. "There are no purring cats, no fishing rods waiting by the door, no baskets hanging from the rafters filled with apples, nor even the blossoms of apples. But these things continue to exist—they are there waiting to tempt us—even if we see them no more!" In silence the girls undressed, taking care—as Sister Purissima instructed them—not to expose any naked flesh.

"This very minute," Sister Purissima continued in unctuous tones, as with a large basket beneath her arm she collected everyone's shoes—shoes they would never see again, as they would be sold to a local orphanage at an outrageous price—"my grandmother is surely making pancakes. The kitchen smells of butter and when a cake falls into the fire she says: See! It is that easy to fall into Hell! And my little sister Bricole is frightened, and her cake, so perfect, golden brown and unburnt, tastes all the better!" The girls had had nothing for supper and the story impressed them. Sister Purissima passed around grey felt slippers: doubly virtuous, they were silent and they kept the floors waxed. For outdoor use each one was given wooden shoes. And then they all climbed into bed—tubercular vaults boxed in on three sides and curtained at the foot, spawning grounds of chronic sleeplessness and nightmares of strangulation, yet proven secure from suitors, thieves, vampires and voyeurs. Then the lamps were all turned down, but for one, for Sister Purissima kept hers as she undressed behind her bed curtain.

Peering from behind her own curtain, Charlotte could see her silhouette, the globes of her breasts jiggling as she brushed the luxuriant hair that beneath the heavy veil of Sisterhood would soon die and fall. Then Sister Purissima prayed. Fascinated, Charlotte looked on, her eyes captured by that voluptuous shadow. Those were the breasts, the thighs of—Wet Winnie! Enchanted, Charlotte longed to burrow between those full breasts like a little white mouse.

That first night, Charlotte dreamed not of Sister Purissima, but instead of Sister Malicia who spanked and patted her until she was as flat as a pancake. And now I'll show you! Sister Malicia said, holding Charlotte-the-pancake to her breast as she approached the grotto of Massabielle transformed into an oven, just how hot it is in Hell!

Towards morning, Charlotte awoke and realized that the air she was breathing was tainted. St.-Gemmes smells! she thought. How can a place devoted to God smell? Everything near her—sheets, blankets, bed curtain—smelled of insecticide and rancid fat. The day before she had noticed that the Sisters all generated a gamy fetor that was almost familiar, like the stench of goats steeping in vinegar. And when Sister Malicia had pushed her face to the floor, Charlotte had felt an unexpected rush of familiarity triggered by her smell. Now, hours later, she made the connection. Sister Malicia smelled very much like Père Poupine, a potent brew of filth and alcohol. Unable to sleep, a triangle of paper in her sleeve, Charlotte made her way to the lavatory, an abhorrent dead end boasting twelve chipped enamel chamber pots. And there in the dim light of dawn she discovered that her nose had not deceived her. For scratched into the pocked plaster beneath the words MALICIA MASTICATES SHIT and MALICIA MASTURBATES (the meaning of this escaped her), she read: MALICIA IS ALWAYS P*I.*A*S*T*E*R*E*D.

Charlotte returned just as Sister Purissima, stomping from one end of the room to the other, proclaimed the break of day by ringing an angry brass bell and clamoring a prayer. The novitiates pulled on their dressing gowns and falling to the floor pronounced in unison the terminal *Amen:*

> *Christ will return,*
> *Christ is here.*
> *Christ will return,*
> *Christ is HERE!*
> *Amen!*

Then in the aquatic gloom of three smoking kerosene lamps, the beds were made, a flea caught and pinched between thumb and forefinger, the dormitory swept, a roach smashed with a shoe; and to the ringing of bells from all quarters, the groggy girls filed, trembling with cold, into the one five-sink lavatory to wash themselves thoroughly with icy water and ash-grease soap without once removing their nightshirts. Indeed, for all the time they would spend at St.-Gemmes, not once would they see a naked body, not even their own. Were it not for relentless hunger, they might have forgotten that they had bodies.

St.-Gemmes supplied two itchy, threadbare, alpaca uniforms, a thin one for winter and a thinner one for the warm weather. Having peeled off their damp nightshirts and dragged on their dresses, the girls filed down three flights of stairs in silence for an hour of prayer in the chapel before breakfast—black bread like boot rubber and a weird substance that might have been embalming fluid and that left in its wake a spoonful of black sand and a heaving stomach.

Here is my body, take and eat!
Here is my blood, take and drink!

CHAPTER
25

Sister Malicia taught History, a noble and theatrical discipline wherein the Rules could be acted out with justifiable rigor. As a young woman she had herself experienced History firsthand. A survivor of cholera and scurvy contracted at sea (in a shipload of Sisters for the Bird, the Adoration and Misery) she had disembarked in China—a hostile and bewildering country where the natives screeched raucously at one another in the palsied languages of parrots—to spread the more dulcet tones of Christianity. During the popular uprisings of the late 1850s, Sister Malicia, who had braved the unbridled rage of the nasty brass imps she despised, paid for her selflessness (or was it her pride?) when her left hand was lopped off by a nearsighted French cavalry officer as he hacked his way into the convent he had been sent to secure. When Sister Malicia got home again, Napoleon III had personally seen to it that her lost hand be replaced by a cunning mechanism of articulated ivory. This handsome object she kept protected beneath a black leather glove.

Charlotte and the twelve other novices in her class all carefully wrote out with rusty nibs and clotted violet ink from the deep wells of their scarred, yellow writing tables upon paper the color of a cadaver the following words: LESSON ONE: DISORDER.

Sister Malicia, her upper body held fast in the viselike grasp of her arms, began:

"Before the pacifying influence of the Church, France was overrun by heathen hordes, diverse and corrupt tribes ruled by pagan princes and their whores, Satanic empires bred of barbarism and insanity. Throughout France insecurity ran rampant.

"Question: What institution brought unity at last to this disorder? Answer: The Church. A. She is the Glue of Unification. B. She is the Glue of Pacification. C. She is the Glue that holds France fast.

"The Church! Torch of Truth! Heroic and Perpetual! Her thousand, thousand worshipers—they too are Glue! Her myriads of saints of both sexes! Glue! D. She is Fusion. E. She is Cohesion.

"It is She who dissipated the pagan night, the shadows of barbarism!"

And then Sister Malicia unfolded her arms, and taking her ivory hand in her good hand, began to turn it around and around on its axis with sharp twists, so that first the palm was visible, then the back. She stepped down from the wood stage that had kept her raised above her class, and addressed a small, dark girl with great, shy eyes and thick brown braids pinned to each side of her head.

"*What* is Fusion?" she asked the child, whose name was Eulalie, the sweat pearling on the dark hairs of her dry upper lip. "*Who* is Cohesion?"

Eulalie was standing so terrified by the manipulation of the hand that she was unable to answer.

"What is Fusion? Who is Cohesion?" Sister Malicia repeated gently, dropping her dead hand to her side while she stroked the girl's silky head with the other.

"Who holds France fast?" she whispered.

Tears dimmed Eulalie's eyes and silently spilled down her soft cheeks. She was trembling.

"You've seen the nettles, you've seen the welts, answer smartly," said Sister Malicia evenly. "If you had been listening like a well-behaved person, you'd know the answer. One last time: Who holds France fast?"

But Eulalie could not answer. Her head was empty of answers. Her head was hollow, a bell without a clapper. Her mind had run down, run dry. Her skull was filled with thunder, and as Sister Malicia dragged her to the front of the class and pulled down her drawers and told her to kneel, facing the stage, she feared her head would explode. She began to shriek to let some air in lest it crack like an over-stuffed sack of bran.

"If you shriek!" Sister Malicia gasped, battling at Eulalie's burning buttocks with the raw, green branches of nettle, "I'll make you stay this way, on your knees for the rest of the hour! Then we will all see at our leisure just how red your bottom is!" She struck again and again with desperate energy as Eulalie began to scream, not so much in pain but with utter terror for her soul, which was in greater danger than her flesh. Charlotte found herself standing, and above Eulalie's shrieks she shouted:

"The Ch-Church! The Ch-Church! The Church is the Fusion and the Eu-Eu . . ."

Sister Malicia dropped the nettles to the floor in astonishment. Leaving Eulalie still on her knees and exposed, she strode over to Charlotte. She was sweating like a mare and Charlotte held her breath against the smell. Yet her anger was nearly spent, and she had had her money's worth.

"You have spoken out of turn," she hissed, flushed with excitement and generally pleased with herself. Then, as the bell rang in the hall to punctuate the hour's passing and the lesson's end she added: "I will punish *you* tomorrow."

The following afternoon Charlotte was told to stand facing the back wall with her arms outstretched and her palms held upright. Upon one hand Sister Malicia placed a Bible, and upon the other an agrarian history of France. As still as a lump of plaster, Eulalie paled as Sister Malicia, having stolen quietly to her side, hovered over her dark head.

"Stand!" she ordered, and Eulalie jumped. "Now, tell me. Who is the Glue?"

Eulalie's teeth were chattering. Stiff as a poker, Sister Malicia stroked the back of her neck with a metal ruler.

It was no accident that Sister Malicia had chosen Eulalie. Very likely any other girl in the class would have had the answer and overcome her fears enough to say it. But Eulalie had been damaged long before coming to St.-Gemmes, and Sister Malicia had instantaneously perceived her unlimited and mouth-watering possibilities. With her metal ruler, she scraped the back of Eulalie's neck, ripping out the delicate hairs, and toyed with her translucent and reddening ears.

"*Who is the Glue?*"

Eulalie was sobbing. All around her girls giggled more or less nervously. At the back of the class, Charlotte clenched her teeth against the gnawing pain in her outstretched arms.

"Go to the front of the class." Sister Malicia nudged Eulalie's spine with the ruler. "And now, what do you do?" Eulalie sneezed, and having sloppily wiped tears and mucus from her face, pulled down her drawers.

"And now?" Eulalie lifted her skirts and fell to her knees. "A lesson well learned," Sister Malicia snickered, satisfied. And for the rest of that interminable hour, Eulalie, with buttocks raised and raw, graced the front of the classroom, and Charlotte, with outstretched arms, the back.

"Lesson Two: Terror. Even the best of glue cannot withstand fire! The united families of Church and Royalty and their realm of prosperity and tranquility were torn asunder by the treason of the rabid masses' vampiric leadership! *The Revolution!* An abomination! France was drowned in blood!

"A. The King and Royal Family assassinated. B. The Clergy crushed or banished. C. The Church, that most noble of patriots, destroyed *in the name of patriotism!*

"Greed triumphed over justice, and in the strangled churches of France infamous orgies were celebrated in honor of trollop Reason! Charlotte, your arms! It was a time of terror, of blasphemy and of *gore!*"

When Charlotte felt that her very soul was embodied in her burning arms the bell rang. She lowered her arms slowly and despite the pain and the fact that she was shaking from head to foot managed to take both books together into her lap without dropping one. Then she walked to the front of the room, and as the others filed out she stood beside the prostrate Eulalie, waiting to be dismissed.

"Did you listen to the lesson?" Sister Malicia held Charlotte by the sleeve. Charlotte nodded. "Then tell me. What was the abomination?"

"The Revolution."

"And who was beheaded?"

"The eu-eu 'ing. Louis 'eize. And his wife. And members of the Church."

"It's a good thing that you listened," said Sister Malicia, "or you would have joined this other hussy up front on your knees with your drawers pulled down."

"I know that," said Charlotte.

"Don't speak unless spoken to," said Sister Malicia. "You'd better learn to watch your tongue. The last girl I had with a wagging tongue was sorry *she'd* spoken out of turn, I assure you. I know how to deal with upstarts. God knows His own, but I know bad blood when I see it, the signature of *Evil!*" And she traced the Stain gently with the sharp edge of her metal ruler. But all at once she cried out in pain, and the ruler fell to the floor with a clatter.

"What was that?" she cried. "What was that! I've been *stung!*" And she beat away at her dress with her good hand. "You go away!" she cried to Charlotte, examining the folds of her dress for an insect. And as Eulalie knelt exposed to the empty classroom, Sister Malicia fell to her knees to

133

explore the floor. But she found nothing; there was nothing to find. For she had simply burned her fingers on the
metal ruler.

That night Charlotte lay awake long after the adorable Sister Purissima had pulled on her nightgown and turned off
her lamp. She reviewed the events of the past two days and
considered the possibility that God had chosen to test her
faith in a singular manner: by placing her in a position
of subservience to a demon of changing aspect. Both her
Aunt Edma and Sister Malicia, so hard, so unbending, so
unmerciful, so alike, were also, somehow, not human, like
totems endowed with terrible powers. If she had been
singled out for sainthood (as she believed in rare moments
of optimism) it was inevitable that her path should be
barred by trials. Yet there was a terrifying possibility: if (as
the Exorcist had described one summer's afternoon in
Edma's kitchen) the world was the construction of Satan,
then she was being tormented not by God to test her faith,
but by Satan—just for the hell of it! And God would betray
her—as He had His son! After all, Charlotte thought, like
Christ—I am flesh! And when the terrible image of the suffering Eulalie flashed across her mind, Charlotte nearly
shouted out loud as her heart chimed in harmony with her
head:

> *Both God and Satan despise flesh!*
> *Both are the enemies of man!*

And then Charlotte saw Wet Winnie shining like a lantern at the foot of her bed, the cow pond a heavenly disk,
spinning beneath her dimpled, ivory knees. Her breasts
trembled as she lifted her hair and gazed intently at her
reflection in the water; to her stupefaction, Charlotte saw
that the reflection in the cow pond was not Wet Winnie's
but that of Mary, the Mother of God.

Her mother's identity had been revealed to her: her mother was the Virgin Mary! To find her, Charlotte need only look into her own heart, and as the vision faltered and passed away, Grace, like a warm ocean, engulfed her. And Charlotte knew that Spirit was the structure of the Universe. That like the phases of the moon, her own heart was subject to its laws. That human destiny, like the crystal structures of minerals, followed a preordained route: each instant of life, each thought, each act, each hunger and dream, was a tiny particle of inevitability treading the path of form and meaning.

But what shape was her destiny meant to take? Once she had eaten glass and had nearly bled to death. Tonight she was certain that this mad act had meant something.

"Mother!" she prayed. "When will my destiny be revealed? O Mother in Heaven! *What does it all mean?*"

A new day dawned on St.-Gemmes, an icy morning, a nauseating breakfast (had Sorberina really boiled the lentils in mud?), interminable prayers, lessons and Rules. (That afternoon, Eulalie had immediately taken position, the paddle replacing the nettles to greater effect, her head periodically ducked into a bucket of cold water.)

CHAPTER
26

Two months have passed and the winds of November howl around St.-Gemmes like packs of famished wolves, as in the forest the scattered beasts themselves, lean survivors of a happier epoch, ululate beneath the racing moon. To conjure both wolf and wind, Sister Purissima burns small yellow lumps of bergamotte, that essence so beloved of Mary.

It is the day before All Saints' Day and the back court gutter is a river of blood. The Mother Superior has hired Père Poupine to help Sorberina slaughter the chickens, and as she holds a chicken fast between her thighs, Père Poupine, his hand steadied with kitchen spirits, whacks off yet another conveniently cataleptic head.

The sounds of frenzied squawking and the desperate beatings of wings, of the inescapable thudding of the ax, of Père Poupine's salty curses, reach the classroom where Sister Malicia defines the Ages of the World:

". . . The Fourth Age is that of Empire," she says, shuffling down the aisles in her worn slippers and turning her ivory hand upon its screw, "wherein the Church reaches out for and embraces the world. It begins with the death of Théodose the Great and extends to the pontificate of Jules III. Throughout this entire period, from 395 to 1503, Satan is held fast in chains at the bottom of the deepest pit in Hell.

"The Fifth Age, from the sixteenth to the eighteenth century, is trumpeted by Satan's escape and the birth of

Protestantism. And the Sixth Age by Satan's second escape and the demonic flowering of the *Freemasonry!*" Fiendish cackles rise from the courtyard.

"And what is the Freemasonry? Edith?" Edith stands. Her back is very straight and she clenches her damp hands piously.

"The Freemasonry is a secret conspiracy."

"Very good. And can you tell us who founded the Freemasonry?"

"Beelzebub!" Edith barks without hesitation. Sister Malicia beams and caresses the delicate pink path that, drawn from forehead to crown, divides the straw-colored hair into two equal parts.

"And the *goal* of the Freemasonry?"

"To . . . to destroy the . . . Christian social order."

"To destroy the Christian social order!" Sister Malicia brays as she strides vigorously back to her desk. "To destroy the Sisterhood! To destroy the Pope! To destroy . . ." and here her voice drops dramatically, "*God*. To destroy *God*. And to establish upon the ruins of civilization, smeared with the blood of saints and baptized babies, *universal Jewish domination!*"

The following day they all ate chicken stew. And mashed potatoes. Miraculously, the potatoes were not burned or salted with sugar. There were carrots in the gravy ". . . and parsley! Look, Charlotte," Edith whispered excitedly, "*parsley!*"

The Mother Superior, who had recently taken to eating in her rooms alone, sat at the head of a long table placed on a stage, along with Sister Malicia and Sisters Clistore, Purissima, Mailloche, Latouche and Inviolata. Because it was a feast day, the Sisters merrily indulged in one of the many pitchers of red wine that Sorberina had set out along with a tempting slice of butter. The novitiates drank an acrid cider liberally cut with water.

Pressed upon by the others, Sister Malicia amused the small party with reminiscences of her life in China.

"The Chinese are obsessive miniaturists," she boomed, greedily sucking the brown flesh from a thighbone. "They spent centuries perfecting methods by which dogs, fish, trees and even the human foot are greatly reduced. . . ."

"A diabolical predilection indeed!" said Sister Inviolata.

"What's worse," Sister Malicia continued, "they do everything *backwards*. . . ."

"*Everything?*" said Sister Inviolata, raising an indiscreet eyebrow.

"They write from right to left . . ."

"If, indeed, those inane scribblings can be called *writing!*" said Sister Clistore.

". . . and rather than remove their hats when they say 'how do you do' . . ."

"They put them *on!*" (This said by all the others amid screams of laughter. They had heard it all before, but this did not lessen their pleasure in the least, quite the contrary.)

"They mourn their dead in white, they blacken their teeth, they eat their vegetables raw"—Sister Latouche pulled at her eyes to give herself a "Chinese expression," and made rabbitlike motions with her teeth—"and their fruit green; drink hot beverages in the summer and keep their coffins at home!"

"There's a *baby* here," Edith whispered to Charlotte. "I've seen it!"

"Where?" Charlotte's voice was muffled. She was keeping the perfect mashed potatoes unswallowed in her mouth as long as possible.

"In the kitchen."

"Whose?"

"The cook's. I watched her nurse it." And putting her mouth to Charlotte's ear she added, "She puts sugar and jam on her titties first!"

"Jam? There's *jam* in the kitchen?" Charlotte reflected upon this for a time in silence. "What were you doing in the kitchen?"

"I was sent by Sister Malicia, for punishment."

"She punished *you?*"

"She says I know my lessons too well and that I must learn humility. I had to peel potatoes." And she held up her hand to show off two nasty blisters, one on her thumb and the other on her forefinger. "These potatoes we're eating, I peeled them."

". . . and they eat earthworms," Sister Malicia continued, "prepared like herrings. And lizards and the larvae of bees. And dogs and rats and for luck the eyes of black cats!"

After lunch the girls were allowed to stroll in the front courtyard. Charlotte noticed that Eulalie was missing and realized that she hadn't seen her at lunch either.

"Edith, where's Eulalie?"

"She's in Sister Malicia's room," Edith answered. "I saw her when I went to tell Sister Malicia that I'd peeled 384 potatoes. She beamed when she saw my blisters! She said"—and Edith imitated Sister Malicia's odd voice— " 'Oh, you *brave* little *martyr!*' And she kissed me on the *lips!*" Charlotte made a face and spat. Edith did the same; then they both spat together and laughed.

"I'll tell you a *secret!*" Edith added breathlessly. "If you promise not to tell in the name of God's suppurating *wounds.* If you tell, God will punish you!"

"God or Pisster Malshittia?"

"Pisster Malshittia!" giggled Edith, drunk with scandal. "Oh *Charlotte!* You know we *shouldn't!*" And her eyes flashed with pride when she said: "I saw Eulalie hanging by her feet from the *ceiling!*"

Around her, contours dissolved, and Charlotte felt exposed, as if an angry eye had probed her intimate self.

But Edith babbled on, proud to have such prodigious information to share.

"Malshittia said, 'Eu-la-lie must pay for her *sins* and pay *again*. Eu-la-lie's humiliation is nice new money for God's pocket!' God's *pocket*, Charlotte!" Edith gasped with hilarity.

"Poor Eulalie!" Charlotte was crying. She and Edith were alone together, behind St.-Gemmes' left wing, and could not be seen.

"Don't *cry!*" said Edith. "Eulalie wasn't crying. Eulalie doesn't *care*. Eulalie doesn't even know where she *is!*"

"What do you mean? What do you *mean* she doesn't even know where she is?"

"Eulalie is *stupid*, Charlotte. Everybody knows that."

"Not that stupid. Nobody is that stupid unless they're dead."

That evening Sister Purissima taught the girls a new song before they went to sleep. The bed curtains open and their dressing gowns on, the girls all sang together:

> *The Church is a GAR-DEN*
> *And Christ is a BEE!*
> *And I am the POL-LEN*
> *For Mary's HON-EY!*

"Suffering," Sister Purissima told them, her hands clutching her perfect breasts, the lovely oval of her face imbued with light, "suffering . . . which repentance transforms to expiation . . . can become a muse."

There must be more to life than this, Charlotte thought, as when getting into bed she recalled those dreamy afternoons with Père Poupine and an image, gold and green, she had seen in the grocery window on a can of sardines.

CHAPTER
27

Once Père Poupine has received his pay (which the Mother Superior counts out into his palm coin by coin in small change), he ambles back to La Folie and Madame Saignée's café, where he spends the evening drinking. Midnight sees him flat broke and reeling down the road to the neighboring hamlets of Louerre and Louresse (where the wolf wanders and where the wolf sleeps), a bottle of rosé wine secured beneath each armpit, the faithful Fleas tagging along behind.

The night is bitter, but the wine kindles a fire in his blood and in his brain that—fanned by the rising winds— illuminates the world like a lantern. He sees each clod of earth distinctly, each stone, each clump of dry grass, as if it were broad daylight and he carried a magnifying glass.

Père Poupine has not read the recent publication by a Monsieur Schwann entitled *Théorie cellulaire* (indeed, he cannot read) and so he is unaware that his body is a fluid fellowship of living cells. And yet, as he stumbles along unassisted by Monsieur Schwann, he sings: "Hé! Fleas! I'm a teeming ca-ra-van!" and:

> *I feel like an am-bu-lant ant-hill,*
> *a-swarm with jiggling ants!*
> *I've got the tail of a meteor*
> *tucked away in my pants!*

. . . Overhead the Milky Way soars and sings; the stars are out and singing for Archange Poupin.

"Hell! I am the stars!" he whoops. "A billion blinkin' fireflies! A billion eyes!" He blinks and the stars wink; he winks, they blink; he turns the cosmos off and on at will.

"Here's to you, brothers and sisters!" He raises his second bottle to the heavens and then, sitting down in the middle of the road, uncorks it with his teeth, holds it to his heart and lovingly nurses it, purring:

"Ah! Little girl, lie down. . . . Ah! She's in love!" Then taking a long, thirsty drink: "Ah! She has fire. Hé! Hé! I knew she would!" And he downs the rest, oblivious to Fleas who nudges his ribs with his cold wet nose and whines, anxious to move on. For he has detected a malevolence brooding in the night.

Suddenly angry, Poupine sends the bottle crashing against a tree.

"*La Garce!*" he yells. "She's empty already! She's left me high and dry! She slipped a devil down my beak, and now my throat's on fire! *On fire!* Fleas! Hé, friend, go fetch me a river. The whole damned sink. I'll drink the fish. . . ." He has trouble pulling himself to his feet.

"Woosh! Wah?" He puffs and wheezes, unbuttoning his pants. "Hé, Water Beetle . . ." he says to his prick. "Why's the wind so salty?" He pees against the sky.

"*De Dieu!* Wet as soup! Dry as ash on the inside! Wet as soup on the outside!"

He feels heavy now, as heavy as a stone, as heavy as a heavy stone in a crucible of stone, in a stone kiln, in the center of the world. . . . He feels the world pressing in upon him on all sides. He falls to his knees, his head touching the earth, his hands hold his breaking head. He is an egg of lead and he is growing smaller, heavier and smaller as the seconds thunder in his ears.

"O bloody hell!" he screams in the dust. "Get me a

drink!" Crabs are scudding within his marrow; a claw prods his liver and his tongue has swollen up like a corpse in the sun.

"*Fils de garce! Plein comme une huître!*"

Poupine stumbles to his feet as his body unscrambles and his swimming head hammers.

"Something wet!" he begs, looking for the river. But the blasted vineyards stretch out into the night forever.

"What happened to all the vines?" he sobs. "And where have all the little snails gone? Little snails!" he calls out, his body racked with fever. "Little grey mares. . . ." But Fleas has seen the wolf; barking, he circles his master, biting his ankles to get him moving, sober him up.

"Fleas! Goddam! Hé!" And suddenly the wolf is there—standing on her hind legs before him, her brass eyes smoldering in her great, shovel-shaped skull, blowing like a steam locomotive, a full two meters tall.

"Bloody Jesus!" She slashes at his face, tearing off his good ear. He screams, flapping his arms madly in the air, his bones jelly and his bowels freezing, a scarecrow buffeted by fear. "Grrrou!"

Fleas rushes at her, showing his teeth, and she dances back, growling and panting. He sees her eyes, those fiery disks spinning in the night; the universe smells of her jaws. Still flapping his arms, Poupine jumps up and down, whooping and clucking like an insane chicken as she circles, pawing air thick with the turmoil of her fantastic breathing, puffing as if she would blow out the moon, a demon of gore and of fire. And then she throws herself upon the dog, and with one terrible bite, rips his neck open. Biting through to the small bones, she throws him over her back and with her head to the side runs on all fours into the trees and disappears.

"*Fleas!*" Poupine turns upon himself gasping for breath, his hand cupped to his bleeding head. "Jesus Christ! Bloody

Christ!" And on disjointed legs he runs as best he can back to La Folie. At four in the morning La Saignée finds him whimpering at her door. She helps him to a chair, cleans his wounds with cognac and then puts him into her best bed. They can both hear her husband snoring across the hall.

"So! You've lost both your ears, and you've lost your dog, Archange? Have you lost your prick as well?"

He moans. She puts her hand down under the covers and feels around.

"Still there!" she smiles, worrying it like the head of a spaniel. "Let's count your blessings. . . ."

CHAPTER
28

Charlotte awoke after midnight. She had been dreaming about Jesus. Like Saint Nicholas, he wore a red mantle and carried a sack. And when he opened His sack, a hot wind—His wind—nearly knocked her over, and the empty sack—His mouth—trumpeted the words:

The Evil must be undone. But as this sentence finished in an echo, Charlotte heard:

The Evil must be undone, done, done, done. And if upon waking she was convinced that Jesus had spoken to her, she was uncertain as to what he had actually *said*.

Unlike the younger sisters, who slept with the novitiates, Sister Malicia had her own room. Or, perhaps, a suite of rooms, cluttered, as were the Good Mother's, with the weird objects that had spoken to her over the years. (Charlotte had seen these and they had fascinated her. The small knob of hard gristle that the Good Mother had uncovered in her soup and that Charlotte had perceived floating in a blue glass jar was not—as it appeared to be—gristle, but, so the Good Mother said, and Charlotte did not doubt her, Godly stuff, dropped in the dish by the invisible beak of the Holy Ghost Himself.)

As Charlotte attempted to picture Sister Malicia's room in her mind's eye, she wrapped herself as best she could in her frayed dressing gown and pulled on two tattered pairs of wool stockings. The air in the room was below freezing, and the chamber pots across the hall were crusted with ice. Charlotte armed herself with her embroidery scissors and slipped out into darkness as fierce as the whale's entrails when it was sleeping with its mouth closed (Sister Purissima).

Charlotte knew St.-Gemmes's every saltpetered crevice by heart and easily made her way down the hall and up the inky, spiral stairs that led to Sister Malicia's lair. But face to face with the invisible door she panicked. A poison apple, the doorknob throbbed in her hand. When at last she turned it, squeezing wasp nest, pins and needles, the door opened with a shriek and Charlotte stood gasping for air upon the worn threshold. She feared she would urinate; she feared she would vomit. Why hadn't she questioned Edith for details? How would she ever find Eulalie in this terrible darkness? And if she found her, would she be able to cut her down with her ludicrous little scissors? And if she *did* cut her down, what would keep Eulalie from crashing to the hard floor head first? What if she killed Eulalie? And if Eulalie was already dead? Would she have to kill Sister Malicia? How? Even if she was only a bag bloated and animated by Beelzebub and not a person, would she be easy to kill? Could mortals kill demons? Would she bleed? Ink? Smoke? And if there was blood! Maybe (Charlotte shuddered), *maybe she is a person after all!* Charlotte would be taken to prison and executed! Her head cut from her body and kept in a basket full of sawdust. As the tears rolled down her cheeks, Charlotte concentrated on her breathing, attempting to take in silent, shallow breaths before entering the room. But as she stood impotent with fear, a match was struck from within the room, a kerosene lamp lit and a face bloomed forth like a moon in the darkness. Charlotte recognized the Exorcist.

"One is born to Glory, Glory is not won; it is the gift of God. Glory is born of silence and of terror (unlike vulgar reputation, which rises like a rocket to the cheers of the vulgar only to fall back with a clatter). Glory, Charlotte, is symbolized by the eagle. And reputation—by the barnyard: the buzzings of shit flies and the cacklings of hens. Glory is born in Heaven. And if legend inflates passing heroes, Glory need not be sung to be seen by God."

"Which means what?" Charlotte asked. It was long after midnight, and she was standing alone in Sister Malicia's room with the Good Mother, who had just spoken, and the Exorcist who was, for the time being, uncharacteristically silent.

"Which means that you, Charlotte, have all the markings of Glory, of—I firmly believe—sainthood."

But Charlotte, driven by anger, dared repeat:

"Which means *what?*"

"Your concern for Eulalie proves the saintly character of your heart. That and the manner in which you have suffered punishment—in silence. And punishment, cruel as it seems, is always just."

"Silence is Divine," the Exorcist cut in, "and speech mundane. The garbled voice of humankind only adds to the general, brutish cacophony of Terra." And he smiled at his little joke. "Saint Paul, whipped thirty-nine times— thirty-nine times on his bare flesh, Charlotte—did not whimper once. Nor did Saint Jacques, for that matter, when they threw him from a terrace. . . ."

"It is the broken bodies," smiled the Mother Superior, "receive the caresses of Christ!"

"Which means *silence!*" said Charlotte. "I'm not to ask: *Where's Eulalie!*" Her sentence ended in a scream. The Exorcist leapt up from the chair where he had been sitting (looking like an undertaker, Charlotte had thought with loathing) and grabbed Charlotte, holding her body fast against his own, and covering her mouth with his gloved hand.

"If you want to see Eulalie," the Mother Superior continued in nurselike tones, "you will have to promise not to scream."

"If you scream again," said Sister Malicia, who had just then appeared from an adjoining room, "you will be severely punished. Screaming, as is trespass, is *against the Rules*. However, I imagine you know that already."

"I don't give a fig!" Charlotte whispered, but loudly enough for all to hear. "I don't give a shit, piss, *fig* for your figgy rules!"

"Charlotte!" The Good Mother was shocked. "Mind your language!"

"Mind your lies!" Charlotte shouted. "Or Jesus will eat you alive!"

For this Charlotte, still held by the Exorcist, received a slap from Sister Malicia. But the Good Mother continued quietly:

"Would you like to see Eulalie now?"

"Yes," Charlotte whispered. She felt her insides crumble into small, brittle fragments. "Eulalie."

Eulalie was in the attic. She was sleeping beneath a heavy wool blanket and when they entered the room, Sister Malicia prodded her body with her foot. Eulalie woke up and opened the blanket, giggling. Charlotte saw that she was naked and that one of her ankles was attached to a chain bolted to the floor. Then Eulalie touched her nascent breasts and began to rub the secret rose between her legs, looking at them all provocatively. Then she laughed, and to Charlotte this laughter was far more terrible than her tears and screams in the classroom had ever been.

"Eulalie is possessed," the Good Mother explained. "The Exorcist is here to cure her. Just as he cured you." Eulalie, down on her hands and knees, was showing them her backside.

"She's got *glass* in her brain," Charlotte wept as they led her away. "Eulalie's brain is bleeding."

"And now, Charlotte," said the Good Mother as they reached Sister Malicia's door, "you will return to bed. You must have faith in Jesus' love and the Exorcist's art. Eulalie will be saved!" But Sister Malicia said:

"Charlotte *did* trespass, and I would like to settle this with her now. I'll send her to bed in due time." And so both the Exorcist and the Good Mother vanished together down the dark staircase, and Sister Malicia led Charlotte back into her room by the ear.

"Now, if you can show me that you have learned this week's *lesson,* I will let you go. And if not—well then, you shall be sorry, won't you!" And as Charlotte stood in the center of the room, Sister Malicia circled her.

"Who invented the guillotine?"

"Do'teur eu-eu-G-oui-oui-tine," Charlotte murmured. The lesson had terrified her, and she had remembered it all. In fact, she had tried, without success, to forget it.

"Yes. And what did he try it out on first? Before it was used *officially?*" (Sister Malicia always salivated when she said the words *official, officially, officer, authority, service* and *sacrifice.*)

"Three eu-eu- c-orpses."

"And does the heart stop immediately?"

"No-no." Charlotte was trembling, and her body, despite the icy atmosphere, was soaked with sweat. "The ventricles may continue to beat for twenty-five minutes."

"And the auricles?"

"An hour."

"You do know your lesson, little Charlotte," Sister Malicia sighed as she caressed the Stain. "Now tell me, what unlikely commodity"—and here she snickered—"was up for sale in the Chinese markets during the famine of 1876?"

Charlotte had stopped crying. An uncanny tingling in all her extremities had given way to a compelling sensation of peace and strength—of rising jubilation. She stared at Sister Malicia's thin, hard mouth, a mouth studded with gold fillings. In the vast, quiet, jubilant space that Charlotte had discovered within herself, she tarried, taking her time with the answer.

"Flesh," she said evenly. " 'uman *flesh*." Charlotte knew that like metal rulers, metal teeth could grow hot and burn. And as she spoke, Sister Malicia clutched her face and screamed, for now her teeth were living coals burrowing into her flesh, and try as she might she could not pull them from her gums. When Charlotte, still poised upon her own private beach of silence, turned and walked away, Sister Malicia, doubled over with pain, did nothing to stop her.

CHAPTER
29

Back home, Edma was making glue. Her kitchen needed fresh paint, the curtains were soiled, the sink badly stained and the air smelled of the dead parts of animals, hoof and skin, that had gone into the fuming pot.

Edma herself was soiled and stained; liver spots speckled her hands and face; she was gaunt and yellow and even crankier than before Charlotte's departure. The Basilica of Bones had become her life. Her organized, aseptic house-hold had toppled; her tight-laced mind had come untied. What little peace and homeliness afforded Emile by the previously ordered routine—mealtimes, baths and naps— had been swamped by Edma's attempt to construct the body she had always furiously denied. But the more she dealt with bones, the more she feared Death; and the more she feared Death, the greater was the Basilica's power; the projection of Edma's own tormented soul, it was entirely evil. And like a leaky coffin it exuded decay.

Emile, meanwhile, tended his cabbages. Cabbages are nearly human, the Exorcist had told him. They stand erect, have heads, and multiply. Emile had always known, had known long before the Exorcist had told him, that cabbages are nearly human, as are all things alive: trees, birds, bees, carrots and peas; the only di-difference, as Emile had ex-plained to Charlotte, is that they are qui- qui- quieter. And it was this quality that Emile cherished. He tended his cabbages, protected them from drought, from winds and frost, kept their ears trimmed and their feet warm—and they, in turn, grew quietly for him. Unlike cucumbers, melons and marrows, cabbages were dark, difficult to digest; if overcooked they provoked flatulence—a thing, said the Exorcist, as odious as fertility.

"Gas and ovulation," the Exorcist liked to repeat, "are humankind's profoundest humiliations."

The cabbages attended to, Emile weeded his parsnips, his leeks and beets. The Exorcist approved of leeks but not of beets and parsnips: those joyless roots entombed in dirt. Even so Emile persisted. On a cold winter's night what could be more heartening than steamed, fresh parsnips browned with bacon, a hot potato salad enlivened with slices of red beet?

"V-v-v-vegetables are qu-qu-quiet!" Emile had said to Charlotte that summer before she had been uprooted from his garden and his life. And Charlotte, who un-un-understood ev-ev-everything, had replied:

"Yes, Emile, I know. Quite. Like the *moon*." Remembering this, and longing for his beloved stepchild, and alone among his silent companions the cabbages, Emile's heart heaved and he bellowed his longing into the wind: *Moo-Moo-M-o-o-o-o-o-o-o-o-o-o-n!*

CHAPTER
30

The Exorcist was in hiding, incognito, and it pleased him. Invisible, he was everywhere. And if the outside world, that fluctuating labyrinth of deceptive appearances, had proved to be too much for him, the convent fitted him like a glass slipper.

For two months the Exorcist, secure within the Mother Superior's cluttered rooms, at home with her little mahogany tables and chairs and pampered on a feminine diet of white-sauced white meats, custard and jam furnished by the mute and indefatigable Sorberina—that stunning specimen of martyrdom (the Exorcist)—had held the pulse of St.-Gemmes at his fingertips. Rooted in the Mother Superior's overstuffed universe, overfed and agitated by steaming, emblematic sexual assaults upon an iron bed blanketed with haircloth, he had feverishly dictated the time, setting clocks forwards and backwards at will, subtly changing the Rules to fancy his moods. It was the Exorcist who decided that the novitiates would, come November, embroider a little red eye upon the seats of their drawers; it was he who bade Sorberina slice the vegetables into cones and pyramids and pepper the feast day cider with a pinch of authentic Spanish fly procured for a price from the ubiquitous Popa dressed as a Berber. And it was the Exorcist— disguised as Sorberina in wig, apron and ratty jersey—who earnestly examined twice daily the palpable essences of 112 virgins in fuming chamber pots, before Sorberina herself appeared to truck them off in a little cart and empty them into the dark hole in the kitchen floor above a vast, abandoned quarry from which many, many years before, stones for the convent's construction had been extracted.

Dressed in Sorberina's clothes the Exorcist was visited with sudden illumination. As a woman not only would he extend himself beyond the limits his virility imposed, but above all he would be far more pleasing to Abraxas. And so Rosa Mystica was conceived, Visiting Sister of the Bird (the name particularly appealing as it implied wings, a beak and claws).

Sorberina removed the Exorcist's beard with wax, a trick she had acquired in her barbaric homeland (she was a Spanish-Moroccan Jew). Under normal circumstances, this was an excruciatingly painful ordeal. But so fired was he by the prospect of his impending transformation, he felt only exultation. Sorberina let out a nun's robes for him and two pairs of ample drawers. He made an imposing nun, gaunt and yellow, so yellow that the Mother Superior agreed to the little powder and rouge he coveted. This proved a cunning tactic, for the others, upon confronting Sister Rosa Mystica for the first time at luncheon, gaped not at her curiously masculine profile, but at those licentiously reddened cheeks. Rosa, for her part, feeling her prick and balls flapping about freely within the soft linen bloomers, felt before her Master the blissful assurance of a virgin who, trembling beneath the opaque gaze of her beloved, knows she is perfectly desirable.

CHAPTER
31

That week the steeple bell changed shape and rang off-key. Having rung the bell herself, Sister Clistore was the first to notice. The Mother Superior assured her that all would soon be put to rights and indeed, shortly after, the Exorcist appeared officially to investigate. The bell had apparently melted sometime during the night, and if before breakfast it proved to be solid, it was still very warm to the touch. He concluded that a malevolent demiurge had squeezed it in his fiery fist from spite.

"Demons abhor bells," he explained to Sister Clistore, who stood eagerly at the foot of the steeple ladder. "As they have unusually large and sensitive ears, their repugnance is comprehensible. The bell cannot be repaired and will have to be replaced."

The mysterious visitor had also mangled Sister Clistore's spectacles.

"I fear," the Exorcist said later, alone with her in the empty dormitory she "kept" (for the novitiates were all at prayer), ". . . I fear that Ialdaboâth, or one of his sons-in-law, is on the prowl." And he stared fixedly down Sister Clistore's exasperated astigmatism. Flushed, she fell to her knees and scrounged around beneath her bed for a tarnished shoe buckle and a bent shoehorn.

"And my gold filling pains me," she complained, eager to keep him beside her. Opening her mouth very wide, she pointed out a questionable molar.

"Life is one long agony," he said, caressing her breasts to ease the toothache and her troubled vision. "And I expect that these small manifestations of Ialdaboâth's unrest are but the clues to greater upheavals to come. Indeed, *upheaval* stirs upon my own lower belly—a certain premonition of chaos."

"O Lord, O Lord!" wept Clistore helplessly. "What am I to do? And this Ialdaboâth: what does he look like?"

"He is a dragon, Madame!" he cried, pushing her down to the floor. "A dragon with his tail in his mouth!" And he held her fast in his embrace and bit her breasts. "Beware, Sister Clistore!" he panted. "He has tarnished your buckle, bent your horn, smashed your spectacles, squeezed your bell and even entered into your mouth! Tonight he is sure to return to accomplish outrages far more heinous!" His hand scuttled up her thigh.

"Mary!" she wept. "What shall I *do?*"

"I have my methods for confounding demons with criminal intentions! How soft you are!"

"Help! Gasp! OmyGod it *hurts!*"

"Pain is at the root of all things!" he sang into her neck.

"*Again!*" she gasped, and then, "again! Again!" But he was—as was his wont—already done.

"Is it *over?*" she wept pitiably. He wondered: *They always weep after.* But said:

"Life, like Pleasure, is fleeting. . . ."

"And Ialdaboâth?"

"My semen has sealed you!"

"Will you—come again?"

"Soon. . . ."

"Ah! *Soon!*" And Sister Clistore embraced the Exorcist heartily.

Briskly, the Exorcist made his way to the Mother Superior's apartments just in time for a delicate breakfast of oysters prepared by Sorberina in compliance with his own precise specifications.

"Oysters," he explained to the Mother Superior as he spooned shallot vinaigrette onto the creatures' exposed and quivering parts, "are simply gorged with good intentions. They mollify Mind." But before he could continue a protracted scream of aboriginal expressiveness pierced the air.

"The attic!" the Mother Superior cried, knocking over her chair in her haste to leave the table. "Eulalie!" Tripping and jostling one another they ran up the pitted stone staircase. The attic door was open and Sorberina had collapsed upon the threshold, Eulalie's breakfast porridge spattering her bodice. Weeping and crossing herself she murmured repeatedly: "Udder of God! Merdiful Mary!"

Eulalie was floating above the attic's bare board floor, her body listing to the left as her chain tugged at her ankle. Her blanket lay in a heap beneath her, and although the attic was freezing she was hot and vapor rose from her breasts and thighs. She gazed down upon them all with an expression of unabashed merriment.

"I am a spider!" Eulalie sang. "I have hair on my legs and *ever* so many eyes! I see your sins eight times eighty and I'm up here eating flies!"

"Get down from there at once!" Sister Malicia pushed the Exorcist roughly aside and threatened Eulalie with a freshly oiled cat o' nine. She struck out, attempting to reach Eulalie's buttocks, but as Eulalie floated in the air just overhead she succeeded only in hitting herself.

"Get down before I kill you!" she screamed as the Mother Superior comforted the sobbing Sorberina.

"I'm a bird!" Eulalie sang. "I'm an angel! I've never been so close to my Lord!" and she roared with laughter.

"She *is* possessed!" Sister Malicia shouted. "The slut!"

"Tetragrammaton!" cried the Exorcist, still clutching a piece of buttered toast. And stuffing it absentmindedly into his mouth, he searched his pockets for a piece of chalk.

"What she needs is a sound whipping!" Sister Malicia muttered between clenched teeth as she attempted once again to belabor Eulalie's bare behind. But Eulalie bobbed out of reach.

"Stand back!" the Exorcist ordered, having at last unearthed the piece of chalk from his pocket. Pulling Sister Malicia out of the way, he began to draw a large circle on the floor beneath the beaming Eulalie. But Sister Malicia would not be quieted and ran back and forth, striking again and again at Eulalie with the whip that tangled by invisible hands slapped her own scowling face.

"Wretch!" the Exorcist shouted. "Now look what you've done!" For the chalk circle was in sore need of repair.

"Demon!" Sister Malicia screeched, throwing the whip to the floor and stamping on it furiously as if it were a snake.

"Silence!" said the Exorcist. He had finished a new circle and was busy chalking in unintelligible assemblages of letters.

"Come down!" Sister Malicia attempted once more, "or I'll whip you into cream!" Sorberina, weeping hysterically, was led away by the Mother Superior.

"Have her rub the doors down with garlic!" the Exorcist called out after. "And I'll need some *dung!*"

"Dung?" Sister Malicia wailed. "What on earth for?"

"So that I may *cleanse* myself!" he shouted, as the screw that had until then held Eulalie's chain to the floor gave way and Eulalie, screaming with laughter and flapping her arms, sailed up to the rafters.

"There is a spider up here!" she cried, delighted. "Just like me!" And to prove this she spread and crooked her arms and legs as her bottom brushed a beam. Sister Malicia scuttled out muttering *poles* and *ladders.*

"O propitious Astarôt!" the Exorcist sighed, captivated by the sight of Eulalie's exposed and plump flesh purse and rosy cyclopean nether eye. "O Athanor of my aspirations, I will exorcise you!" And he gazed at Eulalie in anger and adoration. "And I will have you—you prepubescent priestess! But . . . where was I? Ah! Yes!" He fell upon his diagram to circumvent his circle with a second.

"I've eaten a fly!" Eulalie shouted as Sister Malicia slammed into the attic with a ladder.

"Your time is up!" she cried to Eulalie as she struggled across the room.

"I know what I'm *doing!*" the Exorcist whined, still on his knees. "That ladder is not only useless, it's *dangerous!*"

But Sister Malicia pulled and pushed it towards the Exorcist's rings.

"No!" he cried. "You leave me *alone!* I don't want that ladder here! It will interfere with the formula!" and he stamped his foot. "Ladders are obnoxious to Abraxas! I myself abhor them!" But she was adamant and continued to drag it along the floor.

"I *like* to eat insect meat!" Eulalie sang from the ceiling. Flies, drowsy with cold, slept in clusters on the rafters. The Exorcist had taken position in front of his scrawls with his arms outstretched.

"This is *my* territory!" he bawled. "One step further, Sister Malicia, and I will have to *hit* you! You walk into this circle with a ladder and *anything* could happen!" But she refused to listen. She had vowed to churn Eulalie into butter in the name of all that is holy! And if the Exorcist was said to be an old hand at confronting demons, he shied from contact with Sister Malicia who, as the seconds passed, looked more and more like an enraged lobster. Rather than push her away, he ran around and around his circle with his arms outstretched, calling:

"O Astarôt! Obey promptly! By the Power of the Clavicle! Do not tarry! Come affably!" and so on.

Sister Malicia ignored him and pulled the ladder into the diagram's center. Having climbed it, she stood just beneath Eulalie. Then she reached up as far as she could and grabbed the chain that continued to dangle from her delicate ankle.

"You pull the chain, I'll make it rain!" Eulalie sang. Sister Malicia gave a violent tug and Eulalie, aiming for the bleached and furrowed forehead, urinated.

"You've ruined my rings!" the Exorcist howled, rattling the ladder with such fury that Sister Malicia feared she would be shaken off. Defeated, she climbed back down ranting:

"I'll have you both burned for sorcery!" and she stormed from the room. Her arms folded tightly before her throbbing breast, her head high and her teeth clenched against the wind, she rushed towards La Folie to fetch the priest. Just as she closed the gates behind her, the water pipes all heated simultaneously, and for the first time in the history of St.-Gemmes the breakfast dishes were washed in hot water.

The road from St.-Gemmes to La Folie was made of beaten earth, cracked with cold and slippery with frost. As Sister Malicia skidded along in her timeworn wooden shoes, the bitter November winds hoisted her cloak above her like an ominous sail so that she sallied forth like a pirate ship despite the aggravation of flapping skirts which every tenth step or so bunched and knotted between her legs. Her threadbare woolens did little to protect her and soon she was sneezing into her wimple.

"I'll have them tried for heresy!" she spat into the road. "Flayed for impunity!" And like the clouds that sped above her head, her anger fed upon the wind. By the time she had reached the church she was literally foaming at the mouth.

She found the priest in the sacristy melting down old candles.

"You must come to St.-Gemmes at once!" she cried, her nose and chin flaming. "The place is going to Hell!"

"I am but a simple man!" he whined. All that week he had been harassed, the village haunted by specters: balls of fire, black hens and large moths with skulls grinning on their backs. The day before the Devil's Finger had collapsed.

"I'm all alone!" he complained. "The Exorshist hash dishappeared! I am but a simple man, I assure you!"

"But that is the whole point!" Sister Malicia retorted. "The Exorcist is in St.-Gemmes! It is *he* who has brought this confusion upon us! He doesn't *exorcise* demons—he *conjures them up!*" As it was evident that this information had frightened the poor priest further (he had backed away from Sister Malicia and was dangerously close to the fireplace, indeed the hem of his skirt was dragging in the coals) she tugged at his sleeve and falling to her knees implored him:

"Father! You *must* come! There's a naked novitiate floating in the air as if on water and the bell has been squeezed like a lemon! The visiting nun has an unmentionable the size of my arm and the doorknobs are all on fire!"

"The crucifix!" he cried, gathering courage, and he pulled a whopping brass cross a yard long from the wall. "And holy water!"

As they left La Folie they passed Emile's high garden wall. Behind it, in the company of memories and cabbages, Emile eased his lonely heart by wailing in the wind.

"The whole world has gone to the Devil!" Sister Malicia cried as she pulled her skirts free from her knees. "Since when do the village folk howl like wolves?"

"I thought it was a cow," the priest said. "Mary!"

CHAPTER
32

The Exorcist had taken up residency in the attic. A charcoal brazier flickered at his feet, he was well wrapped in a bear rug; as he consulted a cumbersome set of foxed volumes, Sorberina brought him a fresh pot of nettle tea. As stomachical secretions hinder mental proficiency he refused to partake of anything else.

Eulalie posed an insoluble puzzle. Not one of his grimoires proposed a solution. He had considered and rejected the possibility that her antics were an illusion, a particularly successful example of *hallucination collective*. More troubling, he concluded that the attic door had come to be a freakish crack in the husk of Time; that having stepped inside, one was no more Here, not yet quite There, but somewhere in between. And as even in the best of times—with both feet firmly planted upon reality's relatively trustworthy crust—the risks of demon courtship were manifold and terrible, he shuddered to consider the dangers of such encounters in an attic unhinged from Natural Law.

All morning he had diagrammed the indescribable, evoked with conjurations heathen and uncouth the crown baronets of demondom such as Sabnach and Shax and above all Z'gan who makes fools wise (a likely choice). And when that failed he probed the lesser regions for their valets, the guttersnipes of Hell: Hoi, Ha, Hihi and Hûûû.

In vain. The rascals refused to budge. Eulalie beamed down upon him, shaken by fearless fits of hilarity. And to make matters worse, it was apparent that she was laughing at *him*.

Late that afternoon Sister Malicia appeared with the priest in tow. Blinded by Eulalie's brilliant nudity, he covered his eyes and gasped for breath.

"This is no time for prudery!" Sister Malicia pried his fingers from his face. He saw the heretic sprawled upon his pentacle. Again he brought his hands to his face; then, thinking better of it, let them fall to his sides before bringing them together before his pendulous nose in prayer.

"Let us pray!"

"Not now!" the Exorcist shouted, glued to his diagram. "I've the formula at last! My Lord is sure to come at any moment!"

"Stop him!" Sister Malicia roared. "His Lord is Satan!" And as the priest ignored her and prayed with even greater intensity she shouted, as she prodded the Exorcist with her foot:

"The priest has come to take you to the proper authorities! You will be burned for heresy! You! That hussy in the air! *And* your whore! I am referring to the Mother Superior," she added for the priest's benefit.

Terrified, the priest attempted to extricate himself from such a horrendous responsibility.

"The only authority," he found the courage to utter, "is God." And then, ecstatically, the tears flowing down his cheeks, he added: "A miracle! I am witness to a miracle!"

Sister Malicia left the attic in disgust, and in total frustration growled to the stairs:

"I'll have *both* of them *castrated!*"

She considered going all the way to Rome to fetch the Pope. But at any moment St.-Gemmes would be overrun with demons. Yet the Bishop lived near Angers, only forty kilometers away. Yes! She would fetch His Magnificence at once, bring him to St.-Gemmes and there in the front courtyard, before the sisters, the novitiates and—why not? —the entire population of La Folie, justice would be done, blood would boil and juices flow.

"Juices and Justice!" she repeated to herself girlishly as she trotted on. "Juices and Justice!"

It took her over an hour against the wind to reach the train station—a barren, windswept hovel behind the café where she learned that there was no train for Angers until the following morning. Rather than return to the convent on foot in the cold and dark, an enterprise made impossible by the roaming she-wolf that (she learned only then) had that very week devoured Poupine's ear and his dog, she asked for a room at the café.

She went up to her room at once where she lay on the floor beneath her bed, trembling for her virtue and her life, convinced that the café, patronized by *men,* was inevitably crawling with cutthroats and rapists. When after several minutes of entreaty Madame Saignée managed to convince her to open her door and eat her dinner, La Saignée, her curiosity aroused, asked in as offhand a manner as she could muster:

"Trouble at the Convent?"

"It's too soon for me to speak . . ." Sister Malicia whispered excitedly. "But I'll tell you this much: there's trouble at the Convent only the Bishop himself can put to rights! I'd hoped for the Pope, but you see there just isn't enough time for that! So tomorrow I'll be taking the train"—this said with haughty emphasis—"to fetch him myself. Heads will roll," she added directly into La Saignée's ear, "when His Munificence sees just what's been going on!"

Madame Saignée was impressed, especially as she realized at once just how profitable the situation could be.

"Perhaps you and the Bishop will be stopping here for

refreshment tomorrow evening, after your arduous journey in the train?"

"I assure you," Sister Malicia retorted dryly, "that His Munificence and I will not be traveling by train!" As if, upon reflection, she considered the train a thing unmentionably abject. "We will return to the Convent directly in his *mancelle,* I presume. I have many private matters of the greatest importance to discuss with His Elevated!"

Just before dawn, Sister Malicia—who had twice crossed the ocean—took the train for the first time. And so swept up was she by her Project of Paramount Importance, it did not occur to her that the train might have several stops to make before reaching Angers. And so when after ten minutes it pulled into the minuscule station of a desolate and nameless hole, she got off at once.

The day was both windy and rainy and before she reached the hamlet's drear center, a stone's throw from the tracks, she was already wet. The place was unsuitable for a Bishop—be he ever so humble—and she looked desperately for a large, imposing house. Unable to find it she asked directions of a red-faced hag running for cover with a basketful of bleeding pig lung and a sniveling brood of brats clinging to her skirts and howling for their lunch.

"Madame, if you please, the Bishop?"

"What?" screamed the lady against the wind in the brutish squawk of the local peasantry. She smelled of cow manure. Undoubtedly the entire family slept with the animals for warmth.

"The Bishop. I must speak with him at once!"

"So it's the *Bishop* you're after?" She ogled Sister Malicia most offensively. "Five kilometer down that road there. A big place. Brick. Can't miss it!" And she snickered.

"Cow!" Sister Malicia said under her breath as she turned away.

"Hé! My *sou!*" the cow called after, pulling at Sister Malicia's sleeve. And suddenly she found herself surrounded by the brats, all pulling at her habit and rubbing their snotty faces in her skirts.

"I'll cuff your ears!" she railed, pushing them away. "I refuse to pay for information anybody, anybody at all, could have given!" But the kids clung to her arms and one, a lice-ridden imp of about three, was actually climbing up her leg.

"Off! Get off, you filthy vermin!" she screamed, swatting at them with both hands and giving a little girl with a runny cold sore a kick. "I'll mash you to a pulp!"

And they were gone. She realized only then that their mother had long since disappeared. So had her purse.

"No matter!" she decided, pulling herself together with celerity. "Once finished with St.-Gemmes I'll have the Bishop plough this place under!"

And with that grim notion in mind, penniless and haggard, she set off. Her perseverance was rewarded, for after a long and difficult walk upon a lonely dirt road unruly with brambles, she arrived at the Bishop's residence, an awesome formal structure, imposing and austere. Exhausted, she stood before the gate, not unlike that of St.-Gemmes, and rang the bell. She was kept waiting in the rain for what seemed an intolerably long time; her shoes and the hem of her habit weighty with mud. When at last she saw a great bald-headed person making his way to the gate she called out:

"I've come to see His Highest! You should know better than to keep people waiting!" And as he opened the gate and ushered her in she cried: "Take me to the Bishop at once!"

He nodded, and as he led her gently but firmly towards a filthy room where thirty madmen slavered in chains, she bawled: "The Bishop! The Bishop! There's so little time!"

CHAPTER

33

Ali-Hassan Popa has left Sam La Liberté and Gaufrette alone to share the dubious comforts of Madame Saignée's furnished rooms. Evening finds him in the Convent kitchen, his suitcase bulging with Javanese flyswatters. Having read Sorberina's palm, he tells her that she is lonely, that he'll accept a cup of spiced wine and that dented copper casserole in exchange for the remainder of his stock of dildos, all bottom of the line, but in perfect working condition, surely she can sell them to the sisters for a fat profit? The wine is warming by the fire; its spicy smell kindles a generous mood. Can he bring her a souvenir from Lourdes? He is on his way down from Paris to fleece the Christmas pilgrims and he'll be back by spring. I'm a traveling salesman, he explains, and, he winks, a thief. Both are venerable occupations. A pirate of the byways, his ship skims the silver crests of rich men's pockets. So name your heart's desire, Sorberina! Holy water in exchange for a kiss? A rosary for a whiff of your rose? A cake of lavender soap for a little lather? It's cold outside and life is short and opportunity is fleeting. . . .

Panting, they embrace in the pantry. Monsieur Popa manipulates his rebounding member and a Brazilian dildo with a buoyancy the Exorcist might well have envied. Afterwards, they lie down together upon the kitchen table pulled beside the cooking stove for warmth, and there, for the second time in her life, Sorberina talks. She is worn to the bone! The Good Mother is working her into an early grave! In fact, sometimes she wishes she was already dead, sick to death of cooking and scraping and scrubbing and slicing and fetching and scouring and trotting! And the Exorcist, why—when he's not asking for a gourmet breakfast or to have fancy lace stitched to the hems of his drawers—expects her to find for him the hairy leavings of bats and the whiskers of newborn cats! As if she had the time! Furthermore, the place is haunted: at night her casseroles squeak like mice and hoot like owls, the fork prongs have all gone soft (and she begins to cry), the garden is full of moles and sinking, the chamber pots are leaking, the foundations are rotting, there are badgers in the pantry and demons in the belfry—

"—and in the attic there's garl floatin' in the air!"

"A girl? Floating in the air?"

"Si! Si! Floatin' an' flyin' and larfin' in air!" She clings to Popa like a wet seal. "Tak' me wid you to Rourdes! Do wad you wad wid me! I'll be you slabe! Udderwise I hung myselfd!" To quiet her he massages her oily scalp and whispers candied nothings into her large red ears until she falls asleep.

Levitation? he ponders. And if it is true? What an act! A surefire money-maker!

He had intended to grease his wallet with the sale of a cure for congenital impotency of the follicle. With a little foresight, he could produce a sensational yuletide miracle and never have to deal in banal and ignominious commodities again.

As Sorberina snores, the Exorcist sleeps in the attic, his head propped up upon the *Garbled Mysteries* of Mani. From this ancient bellyache of a book Abraxas hatches and, with claws splayed and savagely screeching, swoops into the Exorcist's dreams, filling the attic with the reek of calcinated horn. Beating the air with his wings, he chases the Exorcist into the Grotto of Massabielle, there where Bernadette in ecstasy drank mud and mortified her tongue with dry thistles. As always when he dreams, his legs are melted butter and molten rubber and he cannot run but stumble and so he slides into the clammy canopy on his belly like a snake. Once inside he recognizes Bernadette's fetid vagina. Mineral incrustations point down from the ceiling like phalli. Others, springing from the floor, thrust rudely against his buttocks or into his navel.

"God knows his own!" Abraxas caws, tearing at the Exorcist's rusty clothes with a cankerous beak. "Hand the goods over else I kobold your bogey for good!"

"Take her!" the Exorcist begs, terrified. And he points up at Eulalie who shines above him like a star. "Take *her!* Not *me!*"

"Sister Rosa has a prick!" Eulalie sings as Abraxas carries her away in his claws. "The prick's nickname is Saint Nick!"

When he awakes in the dim light of the icy November dawn and looks up at the ceiling, he sees that Eulalie is no longer there. Her chain, miraculously unlocked, lies on the floor, but her blanket is gone.

"My Master's rod has hooked the sacrificial lamb!" the Exorcist shouts, and clapping his long, grey hands, he executes a peculiar little jig. "This calls for a celebration!"

But first the convent must be cleansed, the floors and walls washed with vinegar. He'll have to grease some snakes, order sweets, salt the shit, tattoo a pregnant sow, fuck a three-horned cow, burn myrrh . . . he runs down the stairs to the kitchen, falls once, scraping his hands and knees, but no matter—Abraxas has taken Eulalie for *wife!*

"*Sorberinaaa!*" She is huddled in the cinders, clutching Caramelito to her breasts and sobbing.

"Sorberina! I need vinegar—a whole barrelful. And a mop. . . ."

"Binegar!" she wails. "My heart she is broke and he ask por binegar!"

"The floors and walls must all be washed at once!"

"In binegar! Nebar!" And tearing Caramelito from a red nipple, she thrusts him into her basket along with some bread and onions. The Exorcist realizes for the first time that the baby has no legs.

"I go! My hard is broking yet I follow him nomadder!"

"What about breakfast?" he cries, suddenly famished. "And *lunch?*"

"No breakfast! No bunch! *No nodding!* Sorberina—she fed up!" And she slams the door behind her with a vengeance, breaking it loose from its hinges.

The Exorcist scrambles back upstairs, tripping twice in his haste, to tell the Mother Superior of Sorberina's defection. Meanwhile in the lavatory, Charlotte—the Stain on fire—kneads her aching womb, and squatting over one of the twelve chamber pots, *bleeds.* The Virgin Mary, flanked by legions of softly lowing cows, slowly materializes in the dim light, wading knee-deep in an effervescence of what appears to be soda water.

Because Charlotte knows nothing of sexuality, her blood is the unequivocal evidence of God's intention. Weeping in gratitude and terror, she believes she bleeds for Jesus. She is ready, even eager, to bleed to death.

Like a candle flame in a sudden draft Charlotte's vision—so perfect that the smells of fresh dung and grass lie heavily upon the air—sputters and wavers and thins, sliding up to and through the scaly ceiling plaster to appear palpitating with life, just as the Exorcist runs into the Mother Superior's quarters gasping for breath. And as cows graze upon the Persian carpets' scattered birds and flowers, their soft droppings thudding to the floor and steaming at their feet, the Mother of God stares gravely into the Good Mother's shuddering face and, smiling unaccountably, promises *Doom*. Then the vision wanes and eclipsing down between the floorboards trails behind it a thin, tremulous echo:

D
   O
     O
      O
        o
          o
            o
              m

"I've seen the Virgin!" the Good Mother winces.

"Nonsense!" he sneezes. "We've seen my Master! The Virgin has no beak!"

"Those were cows!" she argues. "Not birds!"

"Whoever we saw, the message was clear. . . ."

She bites his neck. "I fear the end has come! Be quick! Bugger me one last time! Then send them—all of them *packing!*"

That morning the Exorcist had seen a large hare racing across the agitated courtyard. It was a bad sign—one of the worst—and he chewed his fingernails fearfully as he looked to the turbulent sky where in the erratic calligraphies of crazed crows he read the fables of imminent disaster. And disaster came. Some said the priest—always a bungler—was to blame, and for a time he kept to the confessional, eating crumbs and trembling for his life. None blamed the Exorcist who, it was generally believed, had moved on to greener horizons months before. Convinced of his guilt, the Exorcist knew better. Had there been enough vinegar, had there been more time, above all had he been *worthy*, it would never have happened. . . .

That morning the air smelled of iodine. Sister Clistore, apparently acting out the part of the missing Sister Malicia, threatened the novitiates into silence with a large saucepan as Sister Purissima whispered blessings and encouragements into every ear, and Sisters Latouche and Maloche crammed them into cow-carts and carriages borrowed *in extremis* from the neighboring farms. Hungry, unwashed and hastily dressed, the novitiates were sent terrified and weeping to their scattered villages and hamlets: Louerre, Louresse, Les Caves, Les Granges, Ste.-Vierge and La Folie. To add to their discomfort they were pinched and squeezed by the horny farmboys and their randy elders whose job it was to see that they all got home before the storm, now visibly rising, hit the valley. Charlotte, a roll of torn bedding wedged precariously between her legs, her cardboard suitcase tucked beneath her feet, was among them. Everyone was going home. Even Sister Rosa Mystica, her unshaven face seeping blue beneath her powder, was seen taking off in the direction of the woods on a velocipede Charlotte had not the presence of mind to recognize.

At noon, Sister Purissima, the last to leave, wrapped some stolen silverware in brown paper and called out her blessings to the Mother Superior who remained mute behind her impenetrable door. If—as the Virgin had foretold—her ship was doomed, she, its captain, was doomed as well. For she was tormented by the thought that for Lust she had abandoned St.-Gemmes and her heart to the ambassador of a new and bitter god.

"May you be witness," she prayed to Jesus, "to this my final act of fealty!"

As Sister Purissima took to the road a great cloud, like a monster bird killed and hung in the heavens, hemorrhaged, bleeding its inky substance across the yellow sky. From that moment the crows huddled together in their nests caw-cawing ceaselessly, their tongues projecting from their beaks as if their little skulls would burst. Bluebottle flies, awoken from their winter slumbers and prodded by static electricity into furious activity, flew into everyone's faces, biting and shitting before miraculously disappearing.

"A sure sign of tempest," said Edma, as standing on the kitchen stoop she looked excitedly to the sky.

"H-h-hail!" Emile agreed. "B-b-big storm!"

As the cow-cart approached La Folie, Charlotte looked out upon the ragged winter landscape. She sat bent over with pain and cold and hunger. Ever since the stigma she had barely eaten, pushing the confines of bodily necessity farther and farther; more than ever she thought of herself as a vessel, empty and attendant. And if the Stain had set her apart, the bleeding, or so she supposed, made her radically different from other girls. Now it was inconceivable that she might marry, give birth. She knew enough to know that her stigma was badly placed.

The pain in her womb was so intense she felt faint. Pain is temporal, she repeated over and over as Sister Purissima had taught her: Without pain there can be no redemption.

Charlotte arrived home just after one o'clock. She found Edma pacing the street, angrily discussing the sky's odd color with an impoverished, habitually bedridden widow whom Edma referred to as "the Ninny."

"A yellow sky means hail," Edma argued. "Every ninny knows *that!*" Edma sent Charlotte directly up to her room.

"I don't want that suitcase cluttering up my kitchen! And get washed, your face is filthy! And your ears!" She poked one with a sharp finger. "I suppose you want to eat. My Lord, the Stain is darker than ever!"

"I'm not 'ungry!" Charlotte cried. The idea of defiling her vessel self with Edma's food, and the thought of the inevitable conclusion, was unutterably abhorrent.

Charlotte crossed the kitchen and from the window saw Emile at the far end of the garden, staring helplessly up at the sky. Lacking the heart and the energy to go to him, she opened the dining room door. All the familiar furniture—chairs, tables and sideboard—had been removed to make space for an accumulation of knucklebones, thigh and wing bones, ribs and the crania of pigs, chickens, cats and crows. Edma's Basilica of Bones, its towers tottering beneath the weight of their own malevolence, brooded delirious in the shadows. Had the Green Dwarf built himself a house—a Temple to Rotten Things—this would be it. Numberless pits and eyes created the impression of pullulating life, of swollen seeds and swollen mouths and swollen appetites. Charlotte hugged the undulating walls and ran up the stairs to her room where she found herself face to face with the furniture. Like fresh corpses, it was draped in white sheets. She fell across the icy bed and pulled an equally icy quilt over herself. Utterly exhausted, she fell asleep at once. In her dreams everyone was floating: Wet Winnie, Père Poupine, the Virgin Mary, Eulalie, floating like tiny kites on strings, and Charlotte feared she would lose them all in the rising wind.

"Tie us to your heart-strings!" Wet Winnie cried as milk spurted from her breasts, filling the sky with rain. "Else we all fly away!" Charlotte's dream evaporated and with a start she awoke. Emile was sitting on the bed beside her. He had been watching her as she slept.

"Li-Little!" he beamed. And he kissed her lovingly on both her cheeks, the one cold, the other burning. "W-welcome *h-home!*"

That night, as rains of salt and ice lashed her window, and overseen by the dolefully humped phantom furniture, Charlotte took a new nib from its silver paper and with her best hand wrote to Marie-Thérèse Papou, Prioress of the Convent of the Thorny Agony in Nevers. Sister Purissima had given her the address that morning.

"It was there that Bernadette died, Charlotte," she had explained earnestly, her lovely eyes flashing. "Marie-Thérèse and I grew up together. Write to her and I for my part will put in a good word for you." The probability that Charlotte would follow in the footsteps of that other chosen child was inexpressibly thrilling.

Dear Mother,
Marked by evil since birth, I have lived in horror of life and dream only of Salvation.

CHAPTER
34

At two o'clock, a fierce and savage wind, a quadruple wind, septuple wind, a wind without rival, leapt from its secret lair in the sky and threw itself upon the vulnerable winter landscape.

The Exorcist, combing the forest for the spoor of venomous mushrooms, reflected that both the immobile air above stagnant pools and the tempestuous spittle of typhoons are expressions of the same breath.

In that ferocious wind the mushrooms—green, bronze, suppurating yellow, orange, black, deadly purple and red— had magically proliferated and all about him fetal knobs and thumbs gleamed phosphorescent and menacing. As he stooped to consider a runny fungus oozing from the mossy crotch of a hideously ancient tree, the sky ripped apart at its southern seams and hail, maturing in minutes from the size of peas to that of turkey eggs, plummeted to earth. Battered and bruised, his clothes ripped to shreds and blown from his back, the Exorcist ran deeper into the forest for cover as trees were stripped of bark and branches, ferns torn from the sod by their roots and mushrooms smashed to a gelatinous pulp that *thwopped* into his face with the consistency of vomited meat. For an hour the land was thrashed by wind and ice as the thunder boomed and the lightning collided convulsively with bells, rakes, nails, pails, chains, lost coins and keys, metal crosses and the tin-tiled roofs of metal sanctuaries. And then it had rained—fresh water, sea water, and even sardines. Why hadn't he gone to her? Pride, perhaps, a recent argument.

"I am surrounded by females," she had complained. "You need not keep your disguise when we are alone together."

"Sexuality is deceptive." He had actually simpered. How unworthy he had been, even of her! "All living creatures carry the promise of both genders. You, my dove, disguised as a cavalry officer, would be irresistible!"

It rained for ten hours and with such ferocity that by nightfall the river had flooded its bank and the countryside lay heaving beneath a seething soup of foul water. In the villages of Louerre and Louresse, desperate families huddled together on rooftops and looked on helplessly as their live-stock and an occasional arthritic ancestor drowned.

The prowling waters lapped at Emile's kitchen garden wall, but it was solid and although he feared for them, his cabbages were safe. But not St.-Gemmes. The ancient quarries beneath the convent were filled with booming tides that like the felines let loose upon the Christian mar-tyrs, ripped into the foundations. Rotten with age, rat nests and saltpeter, they gave way within minutes, and groaning the sacred seed syllable of God's own secret name, Y-O-W-E-H, the entire structure collapsed. Later, when the Exorcist saw the coagulated ruins and knew that his lady and her artifacts lay crushed beneath the rubble, he recalled that Hottentots venerate great stone piles.

Already far from all this turmoil, Ali-Hassan Popa, Sam La Liberté, Gaufrette and Eulalie raced down the bumpy road towards Lourdes at an audacious twenty miles per hour in a spanking *Strassendampfwagen* that Popa had had the cheek to filch at its historic inauguration in Mecklenbourg in 1881. Eulalie, radiant, if somewhat frenetic, was singing at the top of her lungs. Popa had promised her that she would be the star of his next super production, *Prodigious Stupefactions*. As they sped along, Gaufrette sewed silver sequins onto a very small sky-blue leotard.

"This is the *last* time we join the drooping dyspeptics!" Popa yelled above the noise of the motor. "I've had enough of hysteric Christians and their insalubrious silver tainted like a syphilitic prostate. It's not a sanitary way of life; I don't want the kid catching something."

"After Lourdes," said Sam, "I suggest we hit Paris. Do some shows, buy some fancy clothes and four steamship tickets for Quebec."

"Quebec?"

"Why not? I've a cozy cabin in Trois Rivières. . . ." Sam gave Eulalie a wink. "A salmon creek and a sugar tree and . . ."

"And," Gaufrette continued, "a feather bed for Eulalie!"

"Sounds like you've been working this all out," said Popa.

"Are there bears?" asked Eulalie.

"Certainly there are bears," said Sam. "One morning I found a bear bass-baritone sleeping in my bathtub."

"Ooh!" said Eulalie. "Must be a big bathtub!"

"Big enough. Big enough, even, for Ali-Hassan Popa!"

"Phooey," said Popa, somewhat miffed. "What's the good of a big bathtub when the water pipes freeze over?"

"What color's the feather bed?" asked Eulalie.

"It's yellow," said Sam.

"My favorite color," breathed Eulalie.

"Listen, Ali," said Sam earnestly, "there's enough wood in the forest to build ourselves a regular palace!"

"A real sugar tree?" asked Eulalie.

"Truly, Eulalie, nearly all the trees in Trois Rivières are sugar trees."

"Oh Monsieur Popa!" said Eulalie.

"All right with me," said Ali-Hassan Popa, "as long as the folks in Trois Rivières are as gullible as they are in France. . . ."

"Folks are the same everywhere," said Sam.

The Exorcist sat perched in a high tree. A world of water, he beamed, free of spiritual uncertainties. This, he exulted, is the original landscape! In the distance, La Folie lay poised upon the still waters of dawn, as a turd upon a mirror.

He did not consider his position ridiculous. Quite the contrary. For if Yoweh is an eagle and the Holy Ghost a dove, he could well sit brooding in a tree without compromising his dignity. In any case he had no choice; he did not swim.

Crazed with hunger, thoughts of birds led to thoughts of eggs: fried, boiled, scrambled in butter . . . according to the ancient Egyptians, the Cosmic Egg was laid by Keb: The Great Cackler. He sighed, imagining a dish of curried eggs, golden and steaming hot. I must think, he said aloud, of other things. I am paying, or so it seems, for my unbridled gluttony. Tightening his belt and probing his memory, he continued: Maa carries the Cosmic Egg to Khepera the scarab, who rolls it in dung. The Cosmic Egg, he concluded, delighted with himself, like the human spirit, resides in a crust of shit!

Again he looked out upon the waters. But now he wept. Why had it happened? Were the gods prey to madness and disease? After all, he had given his Master a choice morsel for his bed. And he had slipped an entire convent beneath his wing! He and the Mother Superior had, since September, performed the prescribed sacraments, had uttered the ceremonial words and eaten the ritual foods with reverence, had fornicated in the required manner. . . . His stomach sank as a question formed: Had Abraxas, like his mistress, been offended by his female impersonation? Perhaps his Master, far from being seduced, had been—*offended!*

" 'Twas no ignoble travesty!" he cried. "No idle strata-gem! It was only to love you more! To be better loved by you!"

Then he remembered his dream and how frightened he had been when the mineral members had prodded his parts. What a coward he was! He had failed both his lady and his Master miserably.

Perhaps the time has come for him to marry. Since antiquity, a man marries to both please and appease his gods. He thought of Charlotte, now perhaps pubescent, her privates veiled in peachy mists smelling of honey and piss (a pity his tree had not attracted bees!). In what distant isle is the bride rubbed down with coconut oil? Zanzibar? Samoa? His stomach growled, his member stirred.

"*O estôs, stas, stésomenos!*" He who stands, has stood, will ever stand. . . . Embracing a branch he clasps his wand, a pearl poised at its extremity. Spirit cannot be sullied by debauch. One can prostitute matter, never spirit.

"Pan spermia!" he whispers. "Pan spermia!" he cries.

He examines his fingers. A curious substance is seed. So much promise. . . . Once he had faith. . . .

He closed his eyes and remembered those early years, years of hope and of blindness. His own time in Eden. The first consequential dream, the first camera, the first note-book . . . the first creamy page, the purple ink, the feverish hours, those inspired moments. By his own will, by his own hand, the Universe had held. The keys to Past and Future rattling in his pocket, he had witnessed the construction and destruction of Time's sand castles grain by grain. Yes, once the Exorcist had stood upon the navel of the world.

He had lost his most precious possession—his inno-cence. And with it he had lost his pride. Pride of an imagination, of a heart unfettered by doubt, unblemished by failure. With a pang he recalled that instant of clarity when he had chosen to abide by one master. But now—

thrust away and perhaps denied recognition forever—he saw spreading a terrible stain that blotted out his future, poisoning his life.

Dwarfed above the deep he dozed, crumpled like a thing of paper. His sleep was shallow, in truth a half-sleep; like a hook it dredged the dark waters of his memory and he saw, just as he had seen at the summer's end from behind a screen of leaf and bramble, the Téton twins.

At eleven they were still the perfect mirror-images they had been at birth. He noted with glee that one boy's hair was rooted to his skull clockwise; the other's counterclockwise. Lying low in the grasses, an opera glass trained upon them, he gloated over their young flesh, florid and firm; their round buttocks straining against the worn cloth of their breeches as with shouts and laughter they scaled the Devil's Finger. He was still watching when at the end of the afternoon they sat down drowsily together, their golden arms enlaced about each other's waists. How delightful was their eccentric babbling! He inscribed each syllable in a black notebook stained with his sweat and with his seed.

"Kochipilli!" Gontran sang, holding to the sun a jade-green marble flecked with red.

"Kristmax!" Gaston answered, naming his own—an opaque sphere the color of outer space.

"The twinned tongues of Babel!" The Exorcist awoke with the conviction that his Master had sent the long awaited sign. Fully aroused, he reviewed that summer's day once again and like an orange considered it fiber by fiber, grain by grain. Meanings blazed, scorching his heart with the fire of miraculous clarity. *Yes!* The twins had chosen black and green . . . and it came to him, he—whose knowledge of the obscure and the grotesque was incomparable—that the Aztec priests had cut out their victims' hearts with knives of obsidian; that they had named the blood that flowed *liquid jade*. And in a flash he recognized that the twins were the perfect objects of sacrifice, for they were both monstrous and beautiful, and above all they were innocent. Beside himself he crowed from his tree, a rabid rooster receiving the sun. *Who* had led him to Emile's garden shed? *Who* had bade him steal the sharpest of knives? And now, *who* had sent a dream awakening his memory? Who? His Master!

In the milky light of dawn he celebrated above the silver waters:

"Abraxas–Miquiztli! Infinite and perpetual! I will be your knife!" And pulling his spoiled notebook from his wet pocket he scribbled:

> *Ritual Murder is the Absolute Arm of Pleasure.*
> *A Totalitarian Magic! I must invent it!*
> *My Master is a razor of clarity!*

And as the sun slipped up from the water, spinning in the void like an eye above a sewer, he sang out:

"I will be your fishhook! Your High Priest of Appetite!"

He admitted that his life in the convent had been a detour. An enchantment. Only deception. . . .

Exaggerate Aberration, he wrote, *and you will discover Law.*

Was not the Universe a machine of Redemption? And were not its cogs oiled with blood? Invaded with an irrepressible excitement he sobbed: "I shall be redeemed!"

For the rest of the day with a nail he scratched into the bark of his tree, as the waters yet swirled and lapped about his feet:

> *What is Time but a travesty of Eternity?*
> *What is Life but a travesty of Death?*

"O Owl of Hell," he promised, "I will serve you well!" And overcome with emotion and the promise of the great adventure that lay gleaming scarlet in the evening sun, he raised his yellow face to the heavens and called out fearlessly: *Master!*

CHAPTER
35

From the attic window, Emile and Edma looked beyond the kitchen garden wall to where the road, winding from the vines beyond Louerre, dipped into the greasy water.

"Must be plenty drowned down there!" Edma gloated. "Come, come!" she encouraged Emile who at the thought of dead bodies looked terrified. "If we are high and dry, it is because we deserve to be! Well! I'm off to get sugar—there's always a run on sugar in an emergency. And candles. Emile, get the wheelbarrow! Charlotte! Don't dawdle! There's stale bread in the pantry—go and make the soup!" And she gave Charlotte a shove. "Thank God we live on a hill!" Disaster had so lifted her spirits that she hopped downstairs. However, the line-up at the grocery dampened her enthusiasm.

Convinced that they would be cut off from the outside world for weeks if not forever—although the waters were already receding—thirty housewives stood waiting with their brats, their baskets and their buckets.

"Watch it!" whispered La Rouge. "Here comes the Old Fart!"

Edma pulled in at the end of the line and with her wheelbarrow prodded the rubbery thighs of La Fesse, who had the misfortune to be there first.

"Stop pushing!" La Fesse shouted, exasperated. "If you wanted to wee-wee you should have done so before leaving home!" Furious, Edma broke away and with her stony head held high rolled her wheelbarrow down the cobbled street and up to the front of the line—where she was unable to bully her way through.

"I see you coming, Edma!" La Rouge threatened her with an empty oil jug. "Don't you dare try anything!"

"I'm older than any of you!" Edma whined, defeated. By the time she had returned to her place she found herself trailing four newcomers and a scowling boy who, despite slaps from his mother, threw fistfuls of gravel into her wheelbarrow.

Meanwhile Charlotte prepared the evening meal, dizzy with the unreal sensation that seizes those who—their exemplary destiny revealed—consider the uninterrupted parade of daily facts with astonishment. Even as she sliced the onions for the soup, Charlotte was the vehicle of God.

The stigma's pain had ebbed, but the bleeding had not. Yet as the waters withdrew, her own flow progressively waned and presently she knew that it was not God's intention that she die.

Emile stumbled into the kitchen. He was very agitated. With his left hand he tugged at his ear and with his right at the seat of his pants. Charlotte poured milk into the soup and set it at the back of the stove to simmer.

"Ch-Charrrl . . ." He was so excited he could barely speak. "Coo-coo-coo . . . you c-come w-with me to, come w-with m-me to th-th . . . toolshed?"

She took a shawl from her chair and followed him outside.

"What is it, Emile?" She had never seen him so nervous. Emile smiled mysteriously.

Tools and papers littered the floor, and the knives, laid out in neat rows across the blue cloth on the table, were twinkling in the pale light of the setting winter sun that shone in from a small, dusty window. Charlotte, her hair and face rosy in this light, looked very lovely. Emile's heart swelled with pride.

"Ch-Ch-Charlll," he whispered. "Th-these are all f-for you. F-for when you m-m-m-marry. You-rrr d-d-d- your *dowry!*"

"Emile! How? Where?"

"Best quality!" he ignored her, fondling the knives and then tugging at her sleeve:

"L-Look! F-f-f- for fish! These are f-for meat! The b-big one is for s-slicing meat. I-I've l-lost one . . ." he added sheepishly.

Charlotte was crying. "Emile," she sobbed. "I'm not going to marry. Not *ever!*"

"You will marry!" Emile shouted.

"No! I cannot!"

Emile caressed her cheek. The Stain felt soft and warm beneath his hand.

"It does, it does n-not matter!" He was insistent, perhaps angry. "It does not *matter!*" he boomed.

"Emile!" Charlotte had stopped crying. She took his hands and squeezed them. "It's not what you think. . . ." She hesitated. "There's something else . . . I've had a sign from . . ." and she lowered her voice to an almost inaudible whisper, "from *Her.*"

"Her? Her?"

"From the Virgin Mary!"

Emile was breathing hard. His brow was wrinkled with reflection. At last he said, "If you d-d-don't marry, you will, you will stay wi-with Emile! We will grow v-veg-etables together! Look! Look!" and taking a bundle down from a shelf, he unwrapped an enormous red cooking beet the size of a human head. "I-I've invented this b-beet," he said proudly, holding it tenderly with both hands. "N-nobody has ever g-grown such a big-big veg-etable!"

Charlotte put her arms around him.

"I can't stay with you, Emile. I've already written to the Thorny Agony . . . I want to become a nun." And once again she whispered with great intensity of feeling, her sweet, childish face imbued with an eerie luminescence, the sweat pearling on her pale and earnest brow, "You see, Mother Mary has chosen me to be . . . a . . . *martyr!*"

Emile bent over his giant vegetable and sobbed violently. Charlotte went to him and held him tightly in her arms.

"Emile, Emile!" she wept, her heart aching. "I will not forget you. And . . . I will pray for you," she added, all at once inspired. "Every day! Pain is temporal," she reminded them both, parroting Sister Purissima through her tears, "Salvation is eternal."

"E-Eternal!" Emile sobbed. "O mercy, Charlotte! *Mercy!*"

Later that evening the sky cleared and Charlotte looked up from her window at the stars. They looked like wildflowers scattered across a meadow; just as the flowers they seemed to cluster together. Were there great stars, giant stars, she wondered, towering above the others just as trees tower above the weeds? And did the stars have roots? Had they seeds?

In the night Emile fell ill and soiled himself. He was so weak Edma had to undress and wash him. It was the first time she had seen him naked. Scrubbing with savage attentiveness, she discovered that he had only one testicle. And as her own understanding of anatomy was imperfect, Edma came to certain erroneous conclusions concerning the origins of Emile's stutter. By morning Emile felt better and by noon, although his heart was heavy, he was tending his vegetables.

"Y-you won't ever leave me," he said to the cauli-flowers, taking their leaves up gently with splayed fingers.

"M-my babies!" he said to the beets. And to the cabbages he simply said, "My *friends*."

By the following afternoon, the water was gone, leaving behind an afterbirth of mud and muddy debris. At La Folie's sopping skirts, beneath a thin crust of new snow, lay scattered the cadavers of partially devoured cows and horses, mangled carriages and fantastically shaped mounds of straw and wood, tumbled together with filth and clothing.

The rain had swept the village streets clean and the Exorcist breathed in the fresh winter air with hungry gulps. His mood and manner were ecstatic. In the kitchen he found a crust of bread so hard the mice had shunned it; this he gnawed distractedly to appease his hunger as he tore from the worm-eaten shelf a worn and weighty volume bound in suede and printed in brown ink. He threw himself across the kitchen table and, sucking on the bread, leafed through the volume languorously.

The preliminaries, he sighed, are always the best. Within the hour he had refreshed his memory and titillated his imagination.

To think, he salivated (for he was an enthusiastic student of History), that just as the fate of one hundred thousand heretics bubbled and swelled in the open gutters of Castile, the blood of Indians—so angelic they grew no pubic hair—stagnated in the ditches of Montezuma's Mexico like clotted mud!

The Book of Hours, he pontificated to the wall, is a box of knives! And spotting the shadow of his one battered kerosene lamp as it wobbled in the agitated air above his head, he cried:

"I see a bubble of blood hanging there! Now that is a bauble worthy of my child-bride's pretty neck!" He whispered:

I am a murderer. . . . Almost.

. . . And he would make them weep. Their tears would soak the earth like rain.

He sacrificed paper banners, chicken feathers and needles of red coral. He dressed in paper and raved:

"O Perpetual Blood-Clot! O Precious Edge!" Then he slept. Upon waking he took up the knife and held it to his lips.

The days, like sealed envelopes, slipped past. Edma, a burning brick wrapped in rags and held against her icy womb, went to funerals. The more she witnessed, the more certain she was of her own indestructibility. Emile nursed his broken heart and Charlotte prayed: Mère Papou! Mère Papou! Do not exclude me!

Charlotte's bleeding had stopped. She did not know that she would bleed again. She was unaware that she was a woman, and like all women something of a witch, yet she knew that at a precise moment in time she had been given certain powers. In the privacy of her room she attempted to melt the doorknob and bend nails—without success. She believed that it was the stigma that had given her Power.

Her dreams were still haunted by the Green Dwarf. Now that she was certain that the eating of glass had foretold and prefigured the stigma, she assumed that the Dwarf had in his way led her to the Light. Tamed, he appeared in her dreams contentedly suckling the Virgin's quince-shaped teats, or balancing on her draped knee like a ventriloquist's slack-jawed doll.

And then, the letter came, written in a firm, feminine hand on stiff paper. Charlotte stared for a long time at the envelope and the image embossed upon its upper left-hand corner: the Virgin Mary floating within a vertical mouth bristling with thorns. And in a flash that loosened her bones she caught a glimpse of Paradise, those scented paths and immortal lawns of green where pain is as inconceivable as loneliness.

. . . If you are prepared to walk the grievous path of Righteousness, wrote Mère Papou, and to drink the ardent waters of denial, the Convent of the Thorny Agony will gladly receive you.

They wanted her!

The following morning, Charlotte walked to the cemetery and left flowers at her mother's grave. On the broken floor among the scattered glass pearls of a forsaken mausoleum she saw a tramp, his face ravaged by weather and by wine, sleeping. It occurred to her that this soiled rag of a man could have been her father. And that afternoon she packed her suitcase with the two cotton camisoles that already constricted her forming breasts, and several pairs of mended black stockings, all too short for her lengthening legs. At four o'clock Edma and Emile locked the house and walked her to the station. Emile had given her his watch-chain, and she was wearing it around her neck. Although the tracks had been cleared, the train was not on schedule and they had to wait in the icy station for over an hour. No one spoke.

Charlotte was the first to see the train, veiled in a thick mantle of smoke.

Emile gave Charlotte four wet kisses and Edma produced a lethal-looking hatpin with the words:

"Should a man bother you, aim for an eye!"

Now that Charlotte had entered puberty, the Stain had darkened. As Edma stood complaining in the bitter wind, Emile looked desperately into Charlotte's face, shrouded in the misty glass of the train compartment window. To soundless music the dancing hare cavorted on her cheek. How beautiful she was! It is a pity that Père Poupine was not there, for Emile, as ever, was unable to articulate the truth. Yet as the train pulled from the station and

Charlotte's tiny face receded like a falling star, Emile whispered: *Darling.*

Edma and Emile trudged wordlessly along towards home. Now that Charlotte was out of the way for good, Edma was making plans to transform the upstairs room into a copy of the grotto of Massabiele in papier-mâché decorated with lumps of real quartz and moss. She had just seen some quartz alongside the tracks and planned to return with a pail. She did not notice that Emile had turned off into a side street, and when, after a moment, she missed him, she veered about just in time to see him dragging his feet towards Saignée's café.

" 'Mile! Old *fool!*" she scolded, her face contorted in exasperation. "Come back at once!" And wringing her hands: "Where are you going?"

Hunched over, his fists plunged into his pockets as deep as they could possibly go, Emile bellowed into the road:

"G-Going to g-get *drunk!*"

"God give me patience!" Edma crossed herself. "Em-eeeeel!" And lifting her skirts she bustled after him and grabbed him by the sleeves of his jacket. She shook him so violently that his beret fell into the road and when he stooped for it, she gave him a violent kick that sent him sprawling. Violet with rage, Emile slowly pulled himself to his feet. Lifting one knee into the air, he sent an angry fart thundering into Edma's face. Her jaws dropped in disbelief and she stood, vibrating with hatred, her arms shaking at her sides, her fists clenched convulsively. Emile squared his round shoulders and with both hands put his beret on, giving it a jaunty twist. He then executed a mock salute, turned on his heels and shambled off.

"*I-I will be waiting for you!*" Edma hooted after him, the words sopping with the promise of untold disaster.

CHAPTER
36

Clasped in each other's arms, breasts touching, hearts beating as one, the Téton twins clung together. The Devil's Finger had fallen, and with it an elaborate ritual.

Ever since early childhood, the twins, too eccentric to be allowed in school for they continued to soil themselves and were dangerous when separated, had passed their days and their nights beside the stone. There they had contemplated the passage of the sun and moon across the sky and the menhir's forever rotating shadow. Daily meditation from dawn to dusk revealed that, like a marble, the world was round (as were the sun and moon) and that, like marbles, they had been made to spin. The twins invented *Kriegsnatch,* a complex game wherein marbles revolved in varying orbits about one another, but were never allowed to touch.

They dug concentric circles into the earth at the base of the Devil's Finger—which they knew represented the world. And each day, *Kristmax,* the moon (old, Old Black One) and *Kochipilli,* the sun (green, Green Giver) were displaced in an appointed, elegant pattern that was *Kramsda* (invariable) and based on a simple mathematical principle they had discovered exploring the delicate corolla of a flower. In this way the years had passed, and the cosmos had been secure.

But now the world had fallen and they were powerless to

lift it up again. A thousand *Rastatusks* could not have put it on its feet.

For days the twins had wept inconsolably. They knew that soon the sun would be eaten by the moon and that the world would die.

CHAPTER
37

Bolted to the floor with greasy rivets, the iron seats were cold and hard and the air, caustic with coal dust and smoke, scorched her nostrils. Her suitcase clasped to her chest like a shield, Charlotte looked out of the train compartment window. She felt no elation, only sadness.

Two imposing women in fur coats that smelled of pepper sat beside her, ogling the Stain with fixed stares. Charlotte's feet were cold, and when she twisted her ankles to warm them the bones cracked. Both women cleared their throats disapprovingly—one with a mucilaginous grunt and the other with an abrupt, dry snort. Pressed into a corner, Charlotte thought of how the ankle bones were joined to the foot bones, and twisting both her ankles once again wondered what made them crack. She wished that she could momentarily transform herself into a skeleton. Then they would have something to cough and sputter at! Then they would not press so close! She wondered if all saints thought about death quite as much as she did.

Dazed with cold and buzzing disconnectedly, a fly dropped to her wrist. It was half dead and so unbalanced that it persistently toppled over. As it dragged itself on and out upon the back of her hand she watched it with increasing revulsion. Her skin recoiled at the touch of its six viscous feet. Charlotte had always considered the fly to be one of the principle attributes of God. And when it rolled over once again with a maddening buzz, she was submerged with disgust—for the fly, for God, for the oily rivets that held the ugly train seats fast, for the two hulking women and, above all, for herself. And with astonishment, Charlotte realized that she was *afraid*. That she had always been afraid, that it was above all fear, not faith, that was driving her on. Biting her lip, she pressed her forehead to the window. She felt like murder, she felt like suicide, she feared she would vomit, she feared she would explode. The train was passing the forest near Louerre. Splashed with pink, the sky glistened like the throat of a fish. Wood doves flitted from bracken to bushes of copper, and the bones of high weeds rattled their pods menacingly in the wind. All at once the woodlands were infused with an eerie glow, and Charlotte saw, spilling from the shadows, a dappled, golden hare of prodigious size.

In a flash the train dissolved as with unutterable grace the hare vaulted and bounded alongside the tracks in electrifying leaps—arcs of raw energy crackling like hoops of fire as they struck the air. He ran to the setting sun; it floated in the sky like an egg of sugar.

Charlotte sat awestruck, her hands and teeth pressed to the glass, the Stain twitching violently as if it would tear itself free. Fear drained from her heart and in a surge of blind excitement she scrambled to her feet, grabbing on to the loathsome fur coats to steady herself. With a fistful of black and yellow bristles, she ran to the carriage door in time to catch one last glimpse of molten gold—a lightning flash that charged the air with radiance and urgency. Her soul captivated. Delirious.

"Wait!" she cried. "Wait for me!" And she struggled with the heavy brass latch. The two fat women rolled after her shouting. When the door sprang back they grabbed Charlotte by her arms and for an instant she hung suspended over the tracks with one leg wagging in the wind.

She remembered Edma's hatpin. Tearing it from her sleeve, she savagely struck and then, with a kick and a shout of mad laughter, she leapt from the train into the twilight.

When Charlotte's feet hit the earth she goes over spinning and slams into a tree, snapping her arm at the wrist. Clutching it she leaps up and down crying bitterly before crumbling into the underbrush. The scream of the steam whistle brings her jumping once again to her feet. She hears the train creaking to a halt and she runs, kicking up rotted leaves. As she runs the sun sets and the forest is webbed in mist and shadow. Soon all is silent but for the thudding of her heart, her breathing, her footsteps rustling in the leaves and fallen branches.

She smells the hare. His scent falls through the air like the oily petals of roses: sweet, heady, intoxicating. The woods are steeped with it. Ever deeper into the trees she runs, her breath torn from her throat, her arm a burning stone, the pain pushing her on and on . . . and she thinks: So all things are paid for in pain, even now . . . even this . . . terrible *freedom*. The word is written in the stars, the spoor of beasts, the roots of trees; it is written on the face of the rising moon. She looks and sees that the hare is dancing there.

And the moon guides her. A beacon of fire, its flames fall at her feet, igniting a shimmering path through thick groves of mossy trees, wintergreen and holly.

When she can run no more, she squats over the earth, fighting for breath, the sweat pouring into her eyes and open mouth, and rests her arm across her knees. All about her stretches the forest flecked with silver and shivering in the wind. She drinks in the icy air, the sky's deep ocean spitting stars, the pulsing moon.

Charlotte feels between her thighs with her hand. She holds her fingers to the moonlight and tentatively tastes with the tip of her tongue. The stigma, here in the forest! What can it mean? The taste, salty-sweet, familiar, awakens an ancient memory, cherished, yet somehow forgotten, and she sees as if they were once again before her eyes Emile's garden catalogues, those luxuriant images of vermilion tulips in bloom: Break of Day, Scarlet Dream—that opulence she had sought to duplicate with such passionate concentration. How strange, she thinks, that the taste of blood should bring back the smell of pastel, of ink and musty paper! But then, with a shudder, she senses that she is not alone, that someone has crept through the leaves and now stands just behind her. Charlotte tenses, making ready to jump away into the shadows of the trees, when two strong hands reach out and hold her fast.

"No!" she screams, struggling, in fear forgetting pain. "Let me go!"

"*Bon Dieu de bon Dieu!*"

"Archange!"

"What in the name of Hell are you up to, Charlotte? I *thought* there was something unusual skittering about in the woods tonight." When he lifts her into the air she cries out in pain.

"You're hurt!"

"My arm. . . ." Gently he takes her arm across his own and with his thumb and forefinger feels the bones from wrist to elbow.

"It *hurts!*" she shouts.

" 'course it hurts. Bone's cracked for sure. But clean—not too bad. . . ."

"Archange, I've run away. I've *run away!*" she repeats with amazement, giddy with pain and excitement. "I've run away!" she whispers as if to convince herself.

Poupine wears an old cotton scarf tied around his waist; it holds his hunting knife and pistols. These he stuffs down his shirt and with the scarf makes a sling. Then stooping to lift her he sees that her legs are smeared with something dark.

"*Nom de Dieu!* There's *blood!* You're bleeding too!"

"Oh!" Charlotte falls to her knees, blushing. "It's . . ." she whispers, "it's the stigma! Archange, you mustn't tell!"

"Stigma!" He whoops with amazement. "Hah! What nonsense you talk!"

"It's a sign from Mother Mary!" she shouts, furious with him, holding her arm close to her body and rocking from side to side.

"Is that the truth? Had this . . . *sign* before?"

"Just the day of the big storm and I *saw* Her—"

"Charlotte. . . ." He bends to hold her. "We'll talk this over later. I want to get you warm. I've got to take care of that arm."

"I want to talk about it *now!*" He whoops again and lifting her up in his arms he cradles her against his chest and tramps on.

"Rabbit. Now I believe you saw something. I know you *see* things! You're a queer fish," he added, "no doubt about that, a regular mermaiden! Hé! Stop jiggling! But this stigma of yours—well! The moon's full tonight, Charlotte, she was full the night of the flood and I figure, well, likely as not this, hah! stigma only means that you are a normal young female and . . ."

"A female! Archange, what are you talking about?"

"Stop jigging your legs! You can have *babies,* it means."

"You're lying!" Charlotte shouts. "Put me down!" But he holds her close.

". . . Means you're not a seedling no longer, but a full-blown flower. . . ."

"Seedseedseed!" she screams. "I don't want any babies!"

"*Hoolà!* Don't get me wrong! I said you can have them, but you don't *have* to have them! Truth is, Charlotte, you have plenty of time to think it over."

"I'm *not* a female," Charlotte decided. "I'm not a flower!"

"Ah, but you are. You are a wild rose." And bending under a low branch and stepping over a fallen tree he adds, "And here we are!" Behind a cluster of elderberry and hazelnut trees they can see the flicker of firelight.

"Your house!" she squeals with delight, forgetting her anger.

"And yours, daughter, 'long as you please."

"I can stay with you!" It has only just occurred to her.

"*Sûr!* Like a regular outlaw if you want to. Just promise me—"

"I promise!" she shouts before he can finish.

"Promise me you won't break my ears with none of your churchy crap!"

"Oh! Archange!" she wails, angry again; but as he steps over the leaves that have accumulated in drifts at the threshold, she is laughing.

Père Poupine lived in an abandoned troglodyte dwelling that had been carved into the flanks of a limestone cliff centuries before. The other rooms had all collapsed into a pile of crumbly rubble, but his room was solid and dry and a fire blazed in the lovingly carved stone fireplace. The front door was nearly obscured and obstructed by a tangle of vines; and wild onions sprouted in the crevices. The floors were bare stone carpeted only with the dry leaves that the wind had scattered there.

While Poupine prepared the dressing for her arm, Charlotte sat at the stout oak table and admired the room's sumptuous disorder. Medicinal herbs, simples, all gathered, she knew, on the eve of the summer solstice, dangled from three pine broom handles suspended from the ceiling beside the festive garlands of savory autumn mushrooms, threaded together like the caps and boots of fairies. There was also a ham, dusky with woodsmoke, and baskets of chicory and parsnips, nuts and berries and sweet, wrinkled apples hanging from the rafters, safe from the woodmice and the shrews.

The firewood was stacked along one wall, and upon the mantle a kerosene lamp burned brightly.

"If you're looking for liquor," he pushes a redolent bowl of herbs sweetened with wild honey before her, "there's none! None since I lost Fleas from pure, downright . . ." and he makes as if to twist his nose from his head and laughs his gentle, self-mocking laughter, the marriage of a whooping crane and a wheeze.

He tells her his story:

"That wolf was over two meters tall standing on her hind legs and yellow—eyes like sulphur and hungry, stinking hungry, and I was stinking drunk! Why, I'd been seeing things myself—*hallucinations,* got to thinking I was the Milky Way—*De Dieu!* I owe my life to the poor dog . . ." and lifting up his hair, "see, she ran away with my other ear —no matter! I can still hear the deer singing!" And noticing Charlotte's expression of horror—"I don't care, Hell, I've got my sweet life!"

He fetches a basin from the fire and bathes her arm in an infusion of wild basil. Almost at once the pain eases.

"You've a charmed skin, Rabbit! The train picks up speed after Louerre—must have been chugging along near thirty-five kilometers an hour." He then steeps the bandages in a deep clay vessel of herbs and hot water and explains how the essences of the plants enter the blood through the pores of the skin to work a cure.

"Everything in these woods," he says, "is a medicine or a mystery."

"Archange?" Charlotte breathes in the perfumed vapor of the tea. "At sundown I saw an enormous hare—color of gold!"

"Hah! So you've seen the Mystery!" He wraps the cloth about her wrist and arm. "Now there's another queer fish!"

"Queer fish!" she laughs.

"A mythical beast. Like you."

Charlotte stands before the fire and Poupine undresses and bathes her. He gives her one of his own worn flannel shirts to wear: "All I've got, daughter, the other's on my back." With one arm in a dangling sleeve and the other bandaged to her chest, she is so small that the shirt falls nearly to her ankles: like a real nightgown! It smells of him, of smoke and of gunpowder, of sweat, tobacco, the autumn leaves, the entire forest. Enveloped in its warmth she is peaceful. They sit down by the fire.

"Archange?"

"Yes, Rabbit?"

"Tell me about these babies."

"Tomorrow."

"You won't forget? It's important!"

"Damn right it's important. I'm glad to see you're being sensible."

"Archange!"

"Yes, *tomorrow!*"

CHAPTER
38

Emile left the café more miserable than when he had been sober. He did not return home, although the wind sent the drifting leaves whispering and scuttling like crabs at his ankles. Pulling his beret down over his eyebrows, he pushed his clogged feet down the hill past the shuttered grocery and bakery. Leaving the cobblestones behind, he reeled on to the earthen road and out into the windswept, open country.

The full moon, an ominous smudge, did little to light his way. Treacherous stones tripped him and ravenous spaces menaced from the ditch. Emile moaned when the sky stretched and shook itself, scattering icy drops of rain. Unlike his kitchen garden, the Universe was boundless and hostile, forever up to sudden tricks, like this nasty, needling rain. He lowered his head and pressed on—he would not be beaten, the old battle-ax would not see him tonight!

Somewhere he had lost the road and was up to his knees in fermented rubbish and mud. He put his hands to his ears to warm them, and suppressed thoughts of the kitchen fire, the bed halved by an invisible precipice, he shared with Edma. She would be enraged for weeks, the lips of her hard mouth cauterized together as with fire.

Branches scraped in the wind, and Emile imagined that brigands, rubbing their knives together, were preparing to slit his purse and his throat. When the moon slipped from a net of shadow he saw the Devil's Finger lying on its side like an abandoned coffin. Above it the moon was slowly, slowly eaten away by a perfect, black disk, and Emile, in panic and alone, witnessed his first and last eclipse. When in the utter darkness lightning cracked behind his ear, he skittered to the Devil's Finger, and holding his arms out wide, fell upon it like a demented sailor clinging to a whale. Another burst of lightning sent him scrambling to the far side, where he crouched, terrified, but shielded from the full fury of the tempest. And there, drenched to the bone and more wretched than he had ever been in his long, uneventful life, he sobbed himself to sleep.

Once during the night Emile was awakened by a droning in the inky darkness, bewildering sounds like the labored breathing of a fierce animal, of wet cloth tearing; and whisperings in a weird language—a string of convulsive hisses, the fiendish roar and babble of the lunatic asylum and the zoo.

Emile lay pressed into the wet earth, paralyzed, sucked down by a whirlpool of fear, the bewildering sounds bouncing like hard rubber balls in his heart. When the sounds ceased, giving way to the moaning of the trees and high grasses, he sighed, soothed by the wind and his own steamy warmth, and gradually fell into a nameless state of dreamless sleep, a blindness.

When Emile awoke the sun was already high above the horizon. The sky was clear and his clothes nearly dry. He sat up and stretched; every muscle in his body ached and the bones in his spine snapped in bunches. His head hurt so badly he feared the absinthe of which he had partaken so liberally the night before had turned his brains deep green, as Edma had said it would.

Yawning and blinking, Emile scuffled around the Devil's Finger. And on the other side he saw—caught in the claws of the sun—two blurred, pinkish forms sprawling and glistening, crimson, black, nacreous. . . .

Emile rubbed his eyes and looked again, and with a cry stepped back upon the quaking earth. Before him lay the skinned bodies of the Téton twins. Their hearts, cut from their breasts, were missing. Holding his breath he knelt and touched what once had been a face. For an instant his finger stuck to drying lymph. The earth continued to heave and the consistency of the air he was breathing changed perceptibly. Long ago, Emile had overheard Charlotte ask the Exorcist: Where does time go?

As Emile stood over the twins time came to a standstill.

They found him hunched over the bodies, weeping; the murder weapon, Gilles de Rais, plunged into the earth beside him. An investigation of the house and grounds uncovered the entire box of knives. There was no question in anyone's mind that Emile was the murderer. Even Edma was convinced that the liquor had unleashed his dormant demons.

"Never trust a stutterer," La Fesse exclaimed as she pushed a pie across the counter. "The Devil hides his horns beneath a stutterer's tongue!" In a dozen buzzing kitchens it was whispered: "He was always plotting." And Edma, her face a clot of monumental mortification, was heard to repeat time and time again: "The disgrace!" She passed the night on the linoleum on her knees, and the following morning asked the priest to annul the marriage.

"I am still a virgin," she clamored, throwing herself down on the floor and lifting her skirts. "Look! Look!"

Stricken dumb, his eyes glazed over, Emile was taken to a prison cell in Fontevrault where he sat, docile and dribbling, with the eyes of a rotten fish, staring at a dish of congealed, flat beans. And so mindless was his concentration, so absolute his abandon, that as he sat throughout the interminable aeons of the night, the large and small grains of his being, the grist of his marrow and mind, transformed themselves into the blind faces of perfect crystals that multiplied, inexorably, in regular, recurring patterns. And when at last the dawn incised the sky, it was discovered that apoplexy had precipitated Emile into a petrified mass of such rigid density, it took six men and a wheelbarrow to carry him away.

CHAPTER

39

In the morning it is Père Poupine who lights the fire and cooks the wheat porridge in the household's only kettle. Charlotte hears him knocking about, whistling and cussing to himself. She jumps from her bed of ferns and, still warm with sleep, tucks her nightshirt into her leather breeches and new fur vest, both of his making, and pulls on a fine pair of pirated rubber boots. Charlotte says the porridge, sweetened with nuts and honey, is delicious, but he calls it his "Saint Squelcher." Scraped and licked clean, the kettle is ready for the midday stew. Charlotte throws in juniper berries and wild onions along with yesterday's catch of pheasant, and hangs the pot above the fire. Her arm has healed and she passes the day exploring: learning how to read, he calls it, poking and climbing, but also sitting for hours in perfect silence to be rewarded with a long look at a family of foxes nosing for snails in the swollen bark of fallen trees, and a wild sow, swaying and grunting with pleasure as she harvests truffles the size of a fist.

Charlotte memorizes the signatures of animals upon the frost: half-diamond, cloverleaf, crescent and sphere, the patterns of mole-mazes and of mounds, of broken webs and scattered sand. Often he finds her standing with her eyes closed, the shadow of a smile on her lips, smelling the world in the wind, he teases; she says: Listening. When the hare appears again, she wants to be ready. One day she asks: Where are the wolves?

"We won't see any more this winter, daughter, not near cold enough. Mostly they come into the valley from the Gold Coast of Burgundy when the wind is bitter. Should you see the odd one, stand tall. He'll leave you, 'less he's infected. Then there's nothing much you can do 'cept climb a high tree."

"I'd pray!"

"You'd do what I say, climb that tree, yell your head off! And then and *only* then break wind. Pray, sing the Marseillaise—"

They are spying on a rust-red slime. His four black horns, sticky as if freshly varnished, are extended. He nibbles on a fallen quince like a ball of hammered copper. Poupine takes her hand. He says, "We are here!"

Charlotte squeezes his hand, touched by the awe expressed in his simple affirmation of being. She has come to share Poupine's intimate conviction that everything that is, is visible. That the universe is knowable, if only you dare look.

When the looking no more satisfies her, Charlotte draws what she has seen on the limestone walls of their room with bits of charred wood. Her eye is so true, and her hand, that Poupine, thunderstruck, exclaims:

"It's devilish, daughter! Holy, I should say . . ." and they are living in an enchanted chamber, a forest within the forest. The power is such that Poupine complains:

"Can't you put their eyes another way—all those birds and beasts watching me, Charlotte, I can't sleep." Indeed, in the firelight, the walls are all eyes.

"They're only watching over us."

"Bah, needn't mother me! I only meant, well, they breathe and stare—it's uncanny! I can feel their *warmth*." And for a few days he disappears. But when he returns, he has a roll of fine rag paper under his arm, creamy and with a delicate grain.

Charlotte spreads the paper out upon the table and strokes it with her hand. It is soft—like the limestone walls—with an almost imperceptible weave, a texture like pumice or the bark of young trees, of fine silk with a raised nub, she says: The skin of Mystery! And that evening he makes her brushes with the hairs of foxes and the tail of a deer tucked into a reed, held fast with string and candle-wax.

"Give me two weeks, Rabbit—" and he snaps his fingers in the air. "I'll have the colors!"

"The colors!"

A miracle is sixteen cakes of pigment, Charlotte writes in her journal, made of clay and minerals and moss and burned bones and even ground shells. . . . This is the middle of March and when Charlotte stomps in from the woods breathless, her knees all burrs, she sees the gift laid out upon the table. Each cake of pigment is wrapped in silver paper—a gift from the greengroceress!

"Pink," she whispers, unwrapping the first small package. "Carmine."

"Wild rose!" he sings. "Wild rose—my lady's nose!" And he executes a mock waltz around the room with an imaginary partner of gigantic proportions:

> She's way past her prime,
> But she's mine—all mine!

One by one the colors blossom in her hand. Yellow—butter, yolk and saffron; orange—daylily and chanterelle; velvety death trumpet black and sphinx-wing grey. The dark clays, burnt and raw. Tender heart of violet and above all green: copper, mint and grass. . . .

"Today I'll paint a frog!" she cries. "And a . . . or . . . no, I *know!* A stick insect!"

"I know a queen," he begins—

"Color of *green!*" Charlotte pipes in, quick to the game: "Nettle and moss!"

"Thin as a twig, limber and . . ."

"Limber and *lean!*" she shouts triumphantly.

"Too fast for me," he complains, bending over and hobbling about, coughing and sputtering, "it's because I'm old and sick!" And slipping to the floor. "You finish it, child. . . ." He makes a croaking noise. "It's the death croak . . ." he explains.

"Thin as a twig . . . limber and lean . . . Oh! But I *have* it!"

"Damned if I haven't *lost* it!"

"Listen," she laughs. "Limber and lean, she ferries a fern . . . across a clear stream!"

He makes a sour face. "I would have put in something about her being jolly—to rhyme with holly. . . ."

"Sore loser!"

He sits up as if startled and in a high screech, sounding terrifyingly like Edma, he cries:

> *There once was a saint, terribly quaint,*
> *Who ate so much paint, she was ever so faint!*

And Charlotte is at him, all over him, hitting and pounding with her hands and her fists; he grabs her wrists, she is crying, he shouts:

"Hé, *Bondieudebondieudebondieu!* Only *teasing,* Rabbit!" She falls into his arms, sobbing, "Don't, *don't!*" And then, her heart unlocking with a snap: How I hate Aunt Edma still!

From that day Charlotte paints. She paints bats and wasps, thousand-leggers and dragonflies, foxes and crows and crossbeaks. The eaglefern looping from a bed of melting snow, the wild rose, its hairy stems, petals translucent, sunlight catching in the thorns, the whisper of a moth hanging in the air, a snail intimately exploring a leaf. The moon's halo.

She paints frogs swimming in sparkling water, eggs billowing behind like star clusters, tadpoles darting in the maidensilk. She paints the bark of rotting trees, mushrooms blooming in the cracks and a wildcat leaping; a chaos of sharp grasses like whips and knives battered by a furious rain and night owls hunting in the palpitating indigo of the sky. She paints the crossbills scolding in trees of wild cherry, the crisp fruit weighing down the branches and sweetness a vapor in the air. She paints Poupine's face, the sand and gravel of his cheeks and hair, his pale, grey, ironical eyes.

And Charlotte paints the Dancing Hare—his fur ignites in the sun, the long, taut muscles are ready to spring, a spot of moisture shines upon his unutterably sensitive nose. Poupine looks on as she paints in the whiskers with a few swift strokes. And when she dips her brush into the midnight black for the pupils of his eyes Poupine says:

"I don't believe I ever told you how I make that black. . . ."

"Tell!"

He scratches his jowls thoughtfully. "First I take some earth and then some air and then water and: hé, hé! fire, plenty of fire!"

"You forgot something."

"*Sûr!* I forgot something. The cheek of a runaway saint is what I forgot."

"And something else—" Laughing, she pulls Poupine's face to her own and whispers into his ear: "You forgot the star jelly!"

CHAPTER
40

In April, a tiny, grizzled man wearing a cap with earflaps (very like the ones the old Popes used to wear, Charlotte thinks) peeps in shyly at their front door. She is delighted when Poupine introduces him affectionately as "the Pope's Nose." He is surprised to see Charlotte, but in the past week he has seen far stranger things than runaway children.

Poupine invites his friend to sit by the fire. Spitting a rope of black juice into the flames, the Pope's Nose pulls a soft, ugly wad of tobacco from his cheek and sticks it to his bald head, beneath his cap. Roasted potatoes are cooling on the hearth and he stares at them with such longing that Charlotte mischievously grabs one and lays it, still piping hot, in his lap. He shouts and jumps to his feet, sending it rolling to the floor. She catches it and tosses it back. Blowing noisily and licking his fingers, he breaks it into two.

"The mayor sent me," he explains. "He needs you to organize a *battue*."

"Never seen a wolf in this season," says Poupine.

"Not a wolf. Werewolf, more like."

"One little *sou* for the *loup-garou*," Poupine teases. "So, it's a *battue* for beggars! You boys have nothing better to do?"

"This one's different." The Pope's Nose stares at his potato. ". . . Seems it weren't Emile who killed the twins like everybody said."

"*Sûr* it was not he!" Charlotte cries. "Archange and I always knew it!"

"Only thing her uncle ever killed was grubs."

"Three boys were murdered last week," the Pope's Nose continues, "the postman's son and two brothers from Les Caves. They were found with their hearts torn out, guts dribbled all over—dogs did *that,* maybe—" he stops, takes a deep breath, pushes some potato into his mouth, "—and a fourth child escaped, near insane with the terror of it; said the wolf had talked to them, talked about a treasure of gold coins. Said he'd show the boys where it was, said he'd give them a charm, a talisman against the Evil Eye."

"A talisman!"

"When he got home, his mother gave him a beating for lying. Later when we found the bodies, she came telling about the talking wolf. But the boy, he's not talking. Seems he's gone soft in the head."

"*Sacré Vingt Dieux!*" Poupine kicks a log deeper into the fire, sending sparks into the room. "Beat a kid for what he's seen!"

"*Sûr,* he'd been telling the truth! This were no wolf! You see, the next victim was, uh . . ." he bends to Poupine and whispers: "raped."

"Where did you find the bodies?"

"East woods. Yesterday Boiteau sent his son out with the cows, threatened to whip him if he didn't go, the kid were so scared. This morning he found him choked to death with stones and dirt. The bones of his hands were broken— he'd fought like the devil for his life. There was teeth marks. . . ."

"Human teeth. . . ." Poupine has taken out his hunting knife and he polishes it against his thigh. "*Battue,*" he decides. "Easter Sunday. We set off from the cemetery chapel—it's just a short walk from there to Les Caves and it flanks the east woods. Tell the men you trust to come, silent, and before the sun."

"Easter Sunday?" Charlotte wonders. Poupine explains: The choirboys will be taking eggs to the poor in Les Caves, and the path goes through the woods. "Archange? Why does he ask you?"

"He's the best man for a *battue*," the Pope's Nose says, pointing at Poupine with a potato. "Knows the woods better 'n his own arse."

"You've done this before! You've killed *wolves*, Archange?"

"Mad wolves, Rabbit, yes."

"*Hé*, Archange, you might tell me a little story, to keep my mind on cheerful things on my way back home." Charlotte is asleep, Poupine's sheepskin vest pulled up close around her ears.

"I've heard tell of a nun," Poupine begins, "wanting to learn how to fly. . . ." His friend grunts happily:

"I 'specially like it when you tell stories about nuns!"

"Seems she's out meditating on the Good Lord and all that crap," Poupine continues, "in the convent garden. It's spring, she's pretty, she's scared of Satan and she's hopeful as Hell about Paradise. . . ."

"She's got hope in her soul!"

"There's a gardener, strong as a tree, he's come to the convent to seed, and she sees him, and being young and innocent—"

"How young?"

"Seventeen."

"A baby!" he approves. "And?"

"And friendly, she says, with a little voice like bells: 'O *Monsieur*! How I love the springtime! How I love the little birds flying around in the Lord's own sky! How I wish He had given *me* wings!' And the gardener says that he'd be only too pleased to make her some. So he sets to work

213

with some nice, pliable wood, and soon he shows her a handsome pair. He's a poet, *nom de Dieu!* and he's stuck in a flower. She's so pleased, she tries them on at once." Poupine stands up and mincing around on tiptoe, he waves his arms in the air and cries:

" 'O! I'm trying to fly, *Monsieur,* but I can't seem to get off the ground!' " And he takes a few short jumps.

" 'Well—you've got the wings,' he tells her, 'but it's clear you can't fly without a tail. I tell you what—I'll lend you mine!' "

From her bed of moss and leaves, Charlotte lets out a squeal of laughter.

"Hé!" Poupine scolds, "you were supposed to be asleep!"

"Anything the Pope can hear, I can hear! I hope the Pope won't tell my Aunt Edma where I am!"

"I wouldn't tell that old war-horse the time of day," he assures her.

CHAPTER
41

At dawn on Easter Sunday, sixty men come together inside the cemetery chapel. Some carry firearms, but most carry noisemakers: large copper cauldrons, drums and trumpets.

Poupine inspects the guns. He will choose only three gunmen and he wants men and weapons that have already proven themselves. The mayor is the first to step forward. He holds his Remington silver-medal rolling block rifle proudly over his head. The year of the Imperial Exposition he had gone all the way to Paris to buy it, and he cherishes it so much that his wife complains he sleeps with it more regularly than he does with her.

"Mayor," Poupine says, "you close the circle."

Poupine has fifteen gunmen to consider and no one is surprised when he designates the man whose Peabody-Martini has killed two rabid wolves and an arsonist; and the best boar hunter in the valley, a slight, nervous man with lively brown eyes who carries a handsome muzzle-loading Chassepot.

"Nini, you and your *'pot* will open the circle."

Six pistols are loaded with powder and balls of newspaper. These are given back to their owners for noise. Poupine keeps his own Lefaucheux pinfire in his belt.

"Pope, you step over here and read that damned thing, 'stead of chewing on it as if it were a lady's ear."

The little man blushes, pulls off his cap and jams it under his arm. His bald head is stained permanently with tobacco juice. He carries a large, official document rolled up in a tight cylinder. Unrolling it, he drops his cap. He stoops for it, breaks wind, and puts it back on his head.

"Precautionary measures!" he shouts. The men, having heard it all before, groan.

"One. It is strongly recommended that no man participating in the *battue* wear a fur bonnet. Two. Do not fire into the woods, nor leave position under any pretext. Three. No man will shoot at any other animal than the wolf. Uh . . . werewolf," he corrects himself. "Any man to do so will be fined." And he spits copiously into the basin of holy water. The priest is too busy to notice.

"I pray to the bleshed Saint Bonifash. . . ." He sprinkles Poupine with holy water. Poupine jumps back, cursing and wiping off his vest.

"When you see him, shay five *Pater*, five *Ave*. . . ." He stops to push his teeth back into place. "I blesh you!" He hands Poupine a bottle and a cross. "Go in peash!" Archange gives them back.

"You carry them, father!"

"I've my eggsh to dishtribute. . . ."

"Then put your hocus-pocus where I'm thinking." But the Pope's Nose reaches for them and shoves them into his pockets. For luck, he explains. The unused firearms are locked inside the chapel to be claimed only once the *battue* is over. The men grumble, but they know that too many guns spell trouble.

Archange positions his three gunmen in a clearing graced with new grass and clover. Each man is placed twenty, thirty, and forty paces from the next, and each falls at once to his belly: the Remington in the tall grass, the Peabody-Martini in a furrow, and the Chassepot behind a fallen tree. As they take position, the others, still silent, follow

Archange into the woods. The day is so fine that it is hard for many of them to believe that they have come out for murder.

Archange maps a vast circle that circumvents the wood. He hopes that the werewolf will be flushed from the forest and into the open like any hunted animal. A drummer is positioned twenty paces to the right of Nini and his Chassepot, and the last tracker brings the circle to a close twenty paces to the left of the prize Remington. Archange himself climbs into a high oak. It gives him a view of the wood, the clearing and the path that leads from La Folie to Les Caves.

For several minutes the forest, admirably concealing sixty men, is silent. But soon the birds and insects resume their conversations and from everywhere rises a buzzing and twittering that is so carefree and springlike that Archange cannot help but smile. At noon the wind brings the sounds of the church bells and even a faint smell of cooking. He pulls a dry sausage from his pocket, gives it a familiar sniff and dusts it off on his sleeve. He bites into it and chews slowly. Mass is over and in his mind's eye he can see the priest counting out the red-stained eggs into the choirboys' baskets. Leaning back, his face shielded by the heavy leaves, he feels the sap throbbing in the body of the tree, with the sweet, insistent violence of sexual love. The humming of the tree enters into him, his mind drifts and he nods off into a half-sleep. An hour passes and another when a cuckoo calling close by startles him. He stretches and sees that someone is coming up the path.

His breath catches. For now, just beneath him, Charlotte is walking, so lithe and sprightly that her bare feet could be paws. And not far behind her, stalking her, he sees the *loup-garou*. Wrapped in the skin of a yellow wolf, the wolf-head tied to his own like the hood of a cape, the forepaws dangling at his chest, he recognizes the Exorcist. Archange slips

217

from his tree silently and follows as Charlotte, heading for the clearing, picks up speed.

"*La garce!*" he mutters, approvingly. Charlotte continues a few paces further, and then, without warning, halts in her tracks and turns, fists clenched, holding her ground, working her toes into the dust to root herself. The Exorcist walks to her, the wolf-pelt flapping and hissing about him like sinister wings.

"Flame of my life. . . ." He breathes in the scent of her hair and strokes the Stain, but fearfully, something in her eyes he has never seen making him unsure. The word quivers in her throat: *Murderer* . . . a murmur, a purr, the sound charms him. He laughs and takes her arm:

"Ah, *ma chatte!* But there is murder . . . and there is Murder."

Charlotte moistens her dry lips with her tongue. She fears her hatred of him has turned it black, her blood poisoned. He thinks: Her breasts are like little plums, insolent and green. . . . He wants to crush her to him, to enter her, to strangle her, all this and more. She thinks: I must kill time. She says:

"What is the difference?"

"The Ritual!" he screeches. "Power, my heart, veins of my heart . . . I do it for . . ." he whispers: "My Master!"

"Your Master is cruel!"

"Flesh was made for cruelty! And I am His flesh-hook!"

"His flesh-hook?"

"His fisherman!"

"Fisherman?"

"I fish! I fish for flesh!" The wolf-head, its jaws held open with a stick, grins down upon her. He rocks with laughter, and throughout the forest, men sit up and listen. "The race of fishermen lives lawless, like beasts—or angels. . . ."

"Who is your Master? You never told me, only

hinted. . . ." She looks not into his eyes, but into the open jaws of the wolf. He cups the Stain with his palm.

"How He burns! How hot you are, *ma crotte!* Your heart is the heat of the Latent Flame! The moment He leaps forth, the Cosmos will be Fire only; Fire and Night!"

"Name Him!" she insists, working her nails into her flesh; her own palms are in blood, so great is her fear. And now she sees Archange stealing towards them in the trees.

"Baal!" he bleats, the wolf-head swaying from side to side. "But He has other names! Like locusts, so swarm his names!" He fingers her hair. "So fair!" he whispers. And breathing hard, his voice rusty with desire:

"Your body is a blazing pentacle. I have often imagined its five cardinal points." He traces her mouth slowly with his finger. "Your lips!" And brushing her nipples with the back of his hand: "And your breasts . . . your cunt—" he chokes on the word, "and, O *volupté*—your anus! Aggression, my lamb, is an art! The art of desire," he moans. "Desire and death."

Charlotte screams. The Exorcist pulls her body to him; she feels his teeth against her throat, his hand between her thighs. And then Archange is upon them. Shouting, he tears the Exorcist from her body and hurls him into the path. As they struggle, the woods explode with pistol fire and fiends come flying through the light and shadow, drumming and trumpeting; the sounds of holidays and Hell and war.

Archange pins down the Exorcist's chest with his knees. He pulls the grim head back by the chin, exposing the neck, and presses his knife against the vein. A thin trickle of blood runs out from beneath the blade. The knife still held to the wound, he pulls the Exorcist to his feet and with a violent kick sends him reeling down the path. Sobbing, the Exorcist makes for the thicker woods, the blood pissing through his fingers. Everywhere the demons bar his way, slashing at his face with branches of thorn, hacking at the wolfskin with their scythes.

"I am the power!" the Exorcist conjures, his torn hands and face clawing the air: "Shar! Shar! Djar! Djar! Kâ! Ae! Aô!" A wooden shoe hits him in the jaw, cracking the bone. The wolfskin is torn from his back and the clothes from his body. Once he is naked, his tormentors step back jeering, the better to see his nakedness and the blood spilling from his wounds.

"Wolf! Wolf! Show us your teeth!"

"Show us your claws, wolf!"

"Show us your tail!"

"The venom's in the tail!"

"Cut off his tail!"

The Exorcist sees the clearing reflecting peace beneath the sun. Charlotte, hugging a branch to keep herself from falling, looks on as he runs out into the new grass. Raising his battered arms to the sky, he shouts:

"I am—" but his words are muffled by the sounds of rifle fire. Charlotte cries out when the back of his skull explodes.

The three gunmen walk to the body. The Exorcist lies on his back. His mouth is open and a second mouth, hideous and red, bubbles at his forehead. Two choirboys, having just come up the path, approach gingerly, cradling their baskets of eggs. When the smallest of the two sees the body, he shrieks and drops his basket. Archange holds him fast and strokes his hair. The man called Nini, his Chassepot slung at his back, prods the body with his knife. The Pope's Nose pulls him back.

Now the others approach, silent, but for the accidental clang of one copper pot against another. Charlotte looks down upon the men pressing in a ragged circle about the corpse. His body is so thin that from where she stands, high in her high tree, it looks like a pile of gnawed bones. The blood has formed a thickening, glistening pool in the tender green of the April grass. She will always see him thus: the white of his skin, the red of his blood, the green of the grass.

Later, Archange asks her:
    "How did you know?"
    "I knew."
    "Little sorceress!"
    "No! If you only *knew* him. It could only be him. You gave me the eyes, Archange, to see . . . to see how mad he was. Always."

It is in May she sees the golden hare once again. They are both startled, and as she leans above him, nearly swooning with excitement, he crouches in the wood-violets, evoking the treasure at the rainbow's end—a mound of gold and cinnamon and snow—his obsidian eyes transporting her to a swifter, more triumphal star.

He is enchantment. He casts a spell from which she will never entirely awaken, not even when the years will have carried her far from this time and place. And when at last he moves, it is with short, hesitant bounds, as if knotted to her heart by an invisible thread. The witchery is such that when, in an arc of fire, he is gone, she is still leaning. . . .

EPILOGUE

Mère Papou and Sister Purissima are both perplexed. Charlotte has not arrived and there has been no explanation from her guardians. And a package has come for her with no return address.

"Perhaps," says Sister Purissima, "there is a message inside."

"God has permitted me to look into other people's hearts," Mère Papou scolds, squinting with chronically swollen eyes into the perfect oval of Sister Purissima's lovely face, "but has He permitted me to look into their private correspondence?"

"Yet, surely, under the circumstances!" Sister Purissima hesitates. "And there is something decidedly unusual about the package, an odor. . . ." The Prioress lifts it to her nose and makes a face.

"You will find the scissors," she decides, "in the top drawer of the table behind you. Be careful not to drop that bottle of arsenic pills I've been taking for my pains."

A peculiar oily perfume of putrefaction just barely masked by cloves and camphor permeates the air. Within the cured skin of a large, exotic serpent are wrapped two wrinkled, leathery objects.

"Figs!" the Prioress exclaims.

"Rather large, I should think, for figs?" Sister Purissima pokes at them with a timid finger. "Why! These are relics

222

of some sort—mummified flesh. . . ."

"Hearts!"

"But *whose?*"

"Well!" Mère Papou knits her brows. The red-rimmed eyes, festooned here and there with sparse, short, yellow bristles and grains of sand, look thoughtful. "They must be thaumatropes—"

"Thaumaturges?" Sister Purissima gently corrects her. Ignoring her, the Prioress continues:

"I shall put them in the chapel. The head of Jeanne des Anges—who, after all, is not even a saint, although, God knows, she tried her best—is in a sorry state. It should be replaced by these. Jeanne's reliquary is in good condition; the gold leaf is nearly intact."

"But," Sister Purissima ventures, "they could conceivably belong to, well, a king's harlots for example, or—Heaven Forbid!—heretics!"

"Of significant *historical* value in any case. Until we know more about them, I shall have a little marble plaque set beneath with the words: *Hearts belonging to unknown martyrs.*"

"Lovely!" Sister Purissima encourages. "May I suggest we put the new relics just to the left of Bernadette Soubirous' mummified corpse and to the right of the Divine Bridegroom's authenticated Thorn?"

RIKKI DUCORNET is the author of five novels, six books of poetry, a collection of short stories, and two children's books, and has illustrated books by Jorge Luis Borges and Robert Coover, among others. She is also a renowned artist; her drawings and prints have been exhibited throughout the world, including the Museum of Fine Arts of West Berlin, the National Museum of Castro Coimbra, Portugal, the National Museum of Fine Art in Mexico, the Museum of Fine Arts in Lille, France, and the Museum of Ixelles, Belgium.

She has been a Fellow at the Bunting Institute and has received grants from the Ingram Merrill Foundation, the Ontario Arts Council, and the Eben Demarest Trust. In 1993 she received a Lannan Literary Fellowship for Fiction.

She was born in 1943 in Canton, New York, and attended Bard College (B.A. in Fine Art and Medieval History, 1964). She has lived in North Africa, South America, Canada, and France, and for the last six years has been living in Denver, Colorado, and teaching Creative Writing at the University of Denver.